The Mystery of the WILD SURFER

The Mystery of the WILD SURFER

Lee Roddy

PUBLISHING

Pomona, California

MYSTERY OF THE WILD SURFER
Copyright © 1990 by Lee Roddy

Published by Focus on the Family Publishing, Pomona, California 91799.
Distributed by Word Books, Dallas, Texas.

This is a work of fiction, and any resemblance between the characters in this book and real persons is coincidental.

Editor: Janet Kobobel
Designer: Sherry Nicolai Russell
Cover Illustration: Ernest Norcia

Printed in the United States of America

90 91 92 93 94 95 96 / 10 9 8 7 6 5 4 3 2 1

To Betty Depolito, one of the ten top-ranked women surfers in the world; and to Malina (called Marina) Hoshi, a rising young surfer who has won many honors in her native Japan and elsewhere. Their cooperation in granting interviews and providing other surfing information during the author's recent research in Hawaii made this novel possible. If the writer made any errors in this work, they are exclusively his responsibility.

CONTENTS

Chapter One

SUDDEN TERROR

J osh Ladd got himself in terrible trouble in just a few seconds.

The brown-haired, twelve-year-old boy, still dripping wet from surfing, splashed out of the ocean. The beach was deserted. He unfastened the surf cord from his right ankle and left his surfboard at the water's edge.

Tank Catlett, Josh's best friend, called from where he sat astride his board just offshore. "What're you doing?"

Josh raised his voice to answer, "That kid out there's the best surfer I've ever seen! I'm going to shoot some footage of him! Maybe Dad can use some freeze frames* for his newspaper!"

In blue trunks, Josh ran barefoot across the hot sand to the nearby, paved parking lot. It was also deserted except for his father's white station wagon and a black stretch limousine at the far end.

---

*The definition and pronunciation of words marked by an asterisk are contained in a glossary at the back of the book.

The limo had been there when Josh and Tank arrived with Mr. Ladd. All its windows except the windshield were darkened, so the boys had seen no one. Josh and Tank had decided the limo was waiting for the only other surfer there on famous Sunset Beach on the north shore of Oahu.*

Josh heard a car door slam. Though he didn't pay close attention, he realized it was one of the limo's doors. His father was down the beach somewhere taking photos for his weekly Hawaiian tourist publication.

Josh hurriedly reached under the unlocked station wagon's front seat and removed the video camera he'd hidden there. He pulled off the lens cap and ran back across the beach toward the water's edge. There he stopped and hoisted the camera to his right cheek.

"Now," he muttered to himself as he closed his left eye and squinted through the viewfinder with the other, "if that kid'll just catch a wave..."

Josh pushed the "on" button with his right thumb, and the camera automatically focused and adjusted to the light. With his right forefinger, he pushed the wide-angle bar. That gave him an establishing shot showing the location at Sunset Beach.

The camera whirred quietly. The small, black microphone above the lens took in the surf's sound, while the camera captured everything Josh was seeing in the viewfinder.

"Okay," he muttered to the distant surfer, "I'm ready!

Grab a wave!'"

Josh moved his right forefinger to the zoom bar for a close-up. He caught the distant surfer pushing himself up smoothly from a prone position on the board. He stood quickly, knees slightly bent. The boy had no surfing companion, which was unusual.

"Hey, Tank!" Josh called. "He's a goofy foot!" That's what Hawaiians call a surfer who places the right foot forward on the board instead of the usual left foot.

Through the viewfinder, Josh saw the unknown surfer's takeoff. It was perfect. He caught the wave and took the drop to the bottom in the first of four basic surfing maneuvers.

Josh heard the sounds of running feet behind him in the sand. Thinking his friend had come ashore, Josh asked, "Tank, you ever see any kid as good as this guy?"

From offshore, Tank yelled, "Josh! Look out!"

Startled, Josh opened his left eye and glanced up. A guttural voice behind him demanded, "Gimme dat, haole* boy!"

The two-and-a-half-pound camera was snatched from Josh's hands. Two rough-looking men stood before Josh. The one who had seized the camera was brown-skinned, medium height but round as a barrel. He had spoken Pidgin English,* the ancient trade language common to Hawaii's many nationalities.

The taller man was a haole weighing well over two hundred pounds. His broken nose had not healed straight.

A navy blue chauffeur's cap rested on his wedge-shaped head.

"Hey!" Josh protested. "What're you doing?"

The taller man shoved Josh's shoulder, making him stagger backward. Josh was so startled that he didn't have time to be scared. Rather, anger flooded him as the men turned away wordlessly.

Josh ran after them, kicking up fine sand with his bare feet. "That's mine!" he shouted. "Give it back!"

The men turned, their dark brown eyes opening in mild surprise at the boy's daring.

Josh stopped, suddenly aware of what he was doing. "Listen," he managed to say through a mouth that turned dry in an instant, "my dad'll be mad if I lose that camera! How about giving it back, huh?"

The dark-skinned man, who was wearing khaki walking shorts and a blue aloha shirt,* seemed to consider the boy's earnest request. "How'd I get da film out?"

"Tape," Josh corrected without thinking. "Here, I'll show you."

The barrel-shaped man held out the camera. "Any funny stuff and we break da face you!"

Josh nodded, vaguely aware that Tank was splashing ashore, carrying his surfboard. Josh wanted to glance around, hoping to see his father, but he didn't dare take his eyes off the camera. He deftly removed the small cassette. The taller man with the broken nose grabbed it.

The other man handed the camera back to Josh. "No

do dat no moah, or you not be so lucky!"

"What'd I do?" Josh demanded.

Neither man answered. They again turned and walked toward the black limousine.

Josh heard Tank run up behind him. "What was that all about?" Tank asked. Though he usually spoke in an easygoing manner, he was now excited and breathing hard.

"I don't know!" Josh turned to look seaward. The boy he had been videotaping was wading ashore at the far end of the beach. The surfboard was tucked under his left arm. He walked straight toward the limo.

Josh frowned. "He must have seen what happened, but he's not even looking at us!"

"Forget it, Josh!" Tank urged. "We'll never see any of them again."

Over the next several days, the boys discussed the incident countless times with their families and friends. It was decided that the other boy must have been a rich kid, and the two men didn't want his picture taken for some unknown reason.

It was also decided that if Josh's camera had been taken, he would have reported it to the police. But the tape was new and had only a few feet of the unknown goofy-foot surfer. Since there was no real value involved, everybody thought it best to just forget the incident.

Eight days later, the boys were back at the north shore. As before, the area was unusually quiet for late August.

Josh's father dropped the boys off and walked down the beach with his still camera.* The station wagon was the only vehicle in the parking lot.

Half an hour later, Josh and Tank were well out on the water, sitting astride their boards in the manner of surfers waiting for a wave.

Suddenly Josh caught a flash of sunlight off a car's windshield. He glanced toward shore and sucked in his breath. "Look," he said, "it's that same limo!"

Josh and Tank watched as the unknown boy they'd seen before took his board from the long, black vehicle. He walked toward the water and entered. As before, he had no surfing buddy.

"Think we should get out of here?" Tank asked softly.

Josh considered, then shook his head. "No, we've got a perfect right to be here. Anyway, I didn't bring my camera, so those two guys have no reason to bother us. I mean, if they're in the limo."

Tank gingerly rubbed the end of his sunburned nose. It was smeared with zinc oxide.* "I still can't figure out what that was all about."

"Me, either." Josh watched the unknown boy paddling his board toward the surf. "I'm still about half mad over what happened. He'll soon be too far away for his goons to bother me, so maybe I'll go ask him about last week."

"Don't do it! I've got a hunch that if we go near that kid, those men'll be waiting for us when we go ashore! Even if your father's back by then, he's no match for those muscle men!"

Josh sighed. "You're probably right. No sense stirring up trouble. Okay, come on! Let's surf!"

He automatically checked the surf cord attached to his right ankle. The other end of the six-foot, polyurethane tether was secured to a hole in the back end of the surfboard. The cord prevented the board from being swept away if Josh "wiped out."

An inviting wave began building seaward. He shoved himself to his feet and thrust his left foot forward. The right one was back about eighteen inches over the skeg.*

As Josh got his balance, he called, "See you on the beach!"

Josh wasn't very experienced at surfing, so he had a hard time staying upright. He swung his arms jerkily but managed to keep his balance. His wave swept him along at a breathtaking clip. He shot past the third boy riding a separate wave a hundred yards away. The other boy didn't look toward Josh, but Josh saw that he was so good he seemed to be part of the board itself.

Wonder who he is? Josh thought.

Josh stayed up for about twenty-five seconds, the longest ride he had yet made. "Wooee!" he cried, throwing back his head as the wave started to slow. "What a ride! What a—"

His words snapped off as the wave suddenly exploded, then retreated, leaving only a foot of water covering the sea bottom.

Coral heads looked like primitive posts in the totally clear water. Josh recognized glistening, small, black mounds as sea urchins* scattered on the ocean floor.

Josh's board shot out from under him as the sea surged in again. He had wiped out without a chance to do more than suck in a quick breath of air. Instantly, there were about six feet of water under him.

Remembering to stay shallow, Josh landed flat like a sky diver, avoiding the sharp coral. As he sank under the surface, he sensed rather than heard the familiar underwater grinding and turbulence. Then, as he had every time before, he turned his face upward and stroked for the surface.

But something jerked him back. He stroked and kicked hard, stretching his body full length at a seventy-five-degree angle. His right foot was still held fast.

What's happening? he asked himself in surprise. *Why can't I surface?*

He could see the surface just four inches away. He stretched his neck upward and thrust both hands down in powerful strokes to propel himself to safety. But his face didn't move any closer to the life-giving air.

Tank probably can't see my hands or know I'm in trouble! Josh thought. *Got to do it by myself!*

Everything above the water was clearly visible, including the towering cumulus clouds so common to Hawaiian skies. He could see the stiff trade winds pushing them along. Life was there, just inches above the surface, but down here—

Josh shook off the thought. *Don't panic!* he told himself. But that wasn't easy, because something was very wrong.

Out of the corner of his right eye, Josh could see his board standing at a nearly ninety-degree angle, the nose swinging back and forth a few feet away. Ordinarily, it would have shot to the surface and floated there, held close by the cord around his right ankle.

He was suddenly aware that he was very tired. He had been surfing hard, using lots of energy on a ride that had pitched him underwater with a minimum of air in his lungs. Josh desperately needed a breath, and he knew that seconds were precious now.

It's my surf cord! he told himself. *Caught on something. Got to free it—fast!* Turning his head and looking down, he saw that the cord had wrapped around a two-foot-tall coral head.

Stay cool! Josh told himself, keenly aware of the need to breathe. *Pull it free! Pull—hard!*

The cord stretched a little, but the tugging only snugged it tighter around the coral head.

It—won't—budge! Can't get enough slack!

A wave of panic swept over him. He wanted to struggle again and again against the stout cord, even though it was obviously useless. It took all his self-control to think clearly.

Got to go down and free it!

Under ordinary circumstances, Josh could hold his breath for about forty seconds. But he knew he would be fortunate to last even fifteen seconds longer now.

Bending over and reaching for the cord, he felt the sting of salt water and knew he had cut his hands on the living coral. But that was nothing, not if he wanted to live.

Josh tried not to think about the overwhelming need for air. He also ignored the bleeding wounds as he extended his right leg to create some slack between his ankle and the coral head.

When the cord floated a little freely, Josh grabbed it and started to lift it over the top of the coral head. But just then, a passing wave caught him in its strong undercurrent, throwing him backward and badly off balance.

He instinctively started to step down with his left foot. He stopped abruptly, however, remembering the danger of driving sea urchins' terrible spines into his foot.

Next he doubled up as much as his right foot would permit. He shoved the foot toward the coral, again causing the cord to slacken. Then he flipped it, but the current again swept him backward, tightening the cord once more.

Josh had always thought he wasn't much afraid of anything, but he was terrified of what was happening. He needed air so much that he was tempted to suck in even though choking, stinging salt water would have filled his lungs.

Now I lay me—Josh knew he was automatically repeating a prayer he'd learned at his mother's knees. Nearing unconsciousness, he felt a sort of light-headedness seep over him.

Sudden terror seized him as he realized, *I'm drowning!*

Chapter Two

TROUBLE AT HIDDEN COVE

Desperately, Josh shook off the terrible thought. *Can't drown! Got to free that cord! Once more, and this time—get the cord over—that coral head!*

He swung his right ankle close to the mushroom-shaped coral, again causing slack in the surf cord. He reached down quickly and seized the loose billow of line.

Now! With fading strength, Josh lifted the cord over the rounded pillar. *There! It's free!*

He stroked frantically upward. This time, nothing held him back. As his face broke the surface, he gulped air hungrily, but his ordeal wasn't over. He swallowed a mouthful of sea water, coughed, and spit it out. He kept sucking wildly for air but instead getting water that gagged him.

For a moment, I didn't think I was going to—make it, he thought. *So—very tired! Got to get on my board—and—rest!* The waves, he knew, would carry him ashore.

Reaching out feebly, Josh pulled on his surf cord. The waves were pulling the board closer to shore, so it resisted being drawn back.

Finally, Josh's fingers closed on the board, but he didn't have the strength to pull it to him against the sea's power. *Can't—quite—hold it!* he realized. The board slid away.

Josh was well-developed in the upper body and chest from a lifetime of swimming. Yet his strength was almost gone. He hated to think of having to call for help, but he raised his eyes, hoping to see Tank bearing down on him. There was no sign, however, of Tank or anyone else.

Got to do it—myself. One more—time!

He pulled wearily on the cord, bringing the tail end of the board toward him. But as he reached out with his free hand and grabbed for the board, a wave caught it and flung it away.

Oh, no!

Choking in the wave's trough, Josh again pulled on the surf cord. His board started bouncing backward toward him. But his waning strength failed, and he felt the cord slip from his fingers. *I'm—done—for!*

A shadow fell across his face. He glanced up. *Tank!*

It wasn't Tank. Instead, the goofy-foot surfer slid off his board into the water beside Josh.

It was the first time Josh had seen the boy up close. He had dark, curly hair, wide shoulders, a deep golden tan and blue eyes. He was about the same age as Josh and Tank.

"I'll give you a shove across your board," the other boy said crisply. "Try to hang on to it, and I'll get you ashore!"

Josh didn't remember getting ashore. He felt the hot sand under his bare skin as he was stretched out on it. He saw his father dashing across the beach, his camera bouncing crazily from the strap around his neck.

Josh heard his father's anguished voice say, "Josh! What happened?"

"It's okay, Dad," he tried to answer, but no words came. He turned his gaze toward the boy who had rescued him. Josh wanted to say thanks, but instead he closed his eyes and thought of a kid in fluorescent green trunks heading back toward the sea. "Wait!" Josh tried to call, but his father's anxious face was above him.

"Josh! Are you all right? Son, speak to me!"

Josh opened his eyes as his father cradled him. He saw Tank splashing out of the surf, carrying his board under his left arm. On the sand, Tank stopped and bent quickly to release the Velcro fastener from his right ankle. *Why didn't I think of that?* Josh thought fleetingly.

The stranger passed Tank and entered the sea.

As Tank dashed up, Josh managed to say, "It's okay, Dad! Tank! I'll be fine in a minute." He raised his head slightly and looked toward the other boy. "Don't let— him—go away!"

"He's already paddling out," Tank replied. "Just lie still until your father's finished checking you over."

Finally satisfied that Josh was going to be all right, Mr. Ladd and Tank loaded the surfboards in the back of the wagon. Josh, feeling very tired and slightly sick to his stomach, slid wearily into the front seat.

As the white station wagon pulled out of the parking lot for the drive back to Honolulu, Josh saw the black limousine still parked at the far end. The darkened windows prevented him from seeing if the two men were inside.

"Strange!" Josh muttered.

His father sighed. "You scared me half to death, Son!" he said.

Josh nodded as the vehicle started through tall stands of sugarcane growing on both sides of the road. "I was wrong about that kid last week. Got to find him—"

"Save your strength!" his dad interrupted. He paused, then asked, "You sure that was the same kid as last week when those two men grabbed your cassette?"

"Positive, Dad!"

Tank leaned across the back of the front seat, his blond head between Mr. Ladd and Josh. "It was the same kid, all right. Wonder why he took off like that after pulling you out? Didn't give his name or anything."

Josh's father slammed his right palm across the steering wheel. "I can't figure it out! Last week his bodyguards— or whatever they are—threatened you. Then that kid didn't even look at you. Today, he saved your life!"

"I'm just sorry I wasn't close enough to see what'd happened or to help you!" Tank exclaimed. "But when I was running ashore, that kid just walked by me and into the surf. I was so concerned about getting to you that I didn't say anything to him, and he didn't say anything to me."

"I've got to thank him," Josh said weakly.

"How're you going to find him?" Tank asked. "And how do you know those two men won't rough you up if you try to talk to him?"

"I don't, but I've got to try. We'll start by asking Roger and Manuel if they know who he is."

All the boys lived on a dead-end street at the foot of Diamond Head.* Roger Okamoto's family rented an apartment in the same three-story, concrete-block building as Josh's and Tank's families. Manuel Souza's family owned a small, board and batten house* a couple of blocks down the hill.

Neither Manuel nor Roger was home, however, when Mr. Ladd and the boys returned. Manuel's mother said he had gone to visit friends on the island of Kauai.* Roger's mother said he was staying with relatives on the Big Island of Hawaii.

"Well, we can't just sit around doing nothing," Josh told Tank as they returned to their apartments. "Let's go down to Waikiki* early tomorrow morning and ask around. Maybe somebody'll know who that goofy-foot kid is."

"He's too good a surfer to hang around Waikiki! That's only for mainland malihinis!*"

"Maybe so, but it's a place to start. You with me?"

"Always am."

About eight o'clock the next morning, Josh and Tank walked from Diamond Head to the world-famous white-sand beaches about a mile from their apartments.

The lifelong friends were bare-chested, wearing only zoris* and swimming trunks. They carried their surfboards under their left arms as they neared the familiar spot.

Josh glanced down the street to the left. Suddenly he tensed and pointed. "Look! A block away! Isn't that the same stretch limo we saw at Sunset Beach?"

The car was long and black, with a boomerang-shaped antenna on the trunk. The rear and side windows were darkened.

Tank shrugged. "I dunno," he said. "All limos look the same to me. Besides, lots of rich people live in that direction." He swept his free hand toward an expensive Honolulu residential district. "They have lots of limos."

"Yeah, you're right. But what if it *is* the same one? Look, it's stopping!"

A moment later, the huge man with the chauffeur's cap slid out from behind the wheel. The barrel-shaped man got out on the front passenger's side. They glanced around, making Josh freeze.

"Don't look at them!" he whispered, grabbing Tank's arm hard to hold him still. "Maybe they won't recognize us!"

When Josh felt it was safe to do so, he stole a sideways glance down the street. The limo was parked at the curb under some ironwood trees,* but the two men were not in sight.

"Where'd they go?" Tank wondered.

"Let's go see!"

"Josh, they threatened you! Remember?"

"Come on! We'll stay back so they can't see us. Maybe they'll lead us to that kid who saved my life!"

The boys tensed as they got close to the limo. To the left, a grassy park stretched inland toward Diamond Head. To the right, a dense stand of thorny kiawe trees* grew between the boys and the ocean.

"They must've gone in there!" Josh pointed toward the kiawe. One of the impulses that often got Josh into trouble suddenly hit him. "Let's see if we can find them!" he said.

"Let's not!" Tank answered.

"Why not?"

"Because I'm pretty sure I know what this place is! It's the one Manuel and Roger call Hidden Cove. And it's kapu!*"

Roger and Manuel had told scary stories of strange things happening at Hidden Cove. Some locals tended to be superstitious, so Roger and Manuel avoided the area. Up to now, so had Josh and Tank.

Josh scoffed, "Ah, that forbidden stuff is just something the locals say to scare us haoles* away! Come on. We'll stay out of sight. Let's see if those muscle men lead us to that kid!"

Tank flipped his head to throw straight, blond locks from his eyes. His hair was bleached almost white by the

Hawaiian sun. He had again smeared zinc oxide cream on his tender nose, which constantly peeled from sunburn.

"I don't know why I picked you as a friend!" he protested good-naturedly. "I could've had somebody who isn't always talking me into some kind of trouble."

"Shh! Let's hurry!"

The boys searched through the underbrush growing along the outside of the six-foot-high, chain-link fence separating the public from the kiawe. Finally, Josh pointed.

"There! That's the hole in the fence Roger and Manuel told us about!"

"Yeah! Right by that kapu sign!"

Josh glanced briefly at the single warning word and the ancient kapu symbol. It consisted of two crossed staffs with knobs at the top ends.

The boys ignored the sign and crawled through the hole. Josh felt a little tingle at the back of his neck. *Shouldn't do this,* he scolded himself as they passed the sign. *But we'll just go in for a few minutes.*

Aloud he cautioned, "Keep a sharp eye out for those men!"

Josh led Tank along a faint lava trail that obviously wasn't used often. Dry weeds rattled as they passed, reminding Josh of a rattlesnake's warning. He moved on warily, following the trail into the dense, tangled growth of thorny trees. Some were twisted and bent so low to the ground that the boys had to climb over them.

Josh was relieved when he topped a lava mound at the far edge of the trees. He stopped in surprised delight, with Tank beside him.

A small crescent of glistening, white sand was spread out before them. It was about as long as a football field but only a third as deep. Two coconut palms grew close together near the water's edge, their fronds waving in the trade winds. There was no sign of the two men or anyone else.

"Kinda spooky," Tank said softly, glancing around nervously, "in spite of the beauty."

"Ah, you've just been listening to Roger and Manuel's scary stories!"

Still, Josh looked around carefully, too, checking for dangers. All he saw was the secluded area. At both ends of the sandy crescent, ancient volcanic fingers of molten lava had flowed into the sea and hardened into twin, black walls fifty feet high. They totally shut off the area except from the kiawe behind and the open sea ahead.

Tank seemed to have gotten over his concern about the two men. "You ever see anything so perfect?" he asked breathlessly.

"Never! Now aren't you glad we came?"

Josh's eyes lit up with excitement at the sight of two-foot-high, blue green waves running toward shore. They rolled beautifully toward the natural black wall on the left. There they exploded into swirling patches of foam.

Suddenly, Josh tensed. "Listen! Somebody's coming!"

He glanced around nervously, expecting to see the two muscle men rushing up on them. Instead, about fifty feet to the right, a tall boy in fluorescent green shorts and zoris emerged from the kiawe trees. He carried a surfboard covered with colorful stickers.

"That's him!" Josh exclaimed.

"You're right. But where are those two men?"

"I don't see them. Come on! I'll go thank that kid!"

"Then can we get out of here?"

"Okay," Josh said with a nod. "I thank him, then we leave."

The friends hurried across the beach to intercept the other boy. He was slender at the waist, with well-developed upper arms. He was about an inch taller than Josh and Tank, and he strode purposefully toward the water's edge, apparently not noticing their approach.

Something about the third boy's strong, easy walk suggested independence and confidence. The way he carried his surfboard also hinted that he was a person who could walk alone, without bodyguards.

"Hi!" Josh called, waving his free hand.

The stranger stopped abruptly and looked up. His blue eyes registered surprise.

Josh and Tank stopped a few feet in front of him. "Aren't you the guy who pulled me out of the surf at Sunset?" Josh asked.

"I was there," the boy replied noncommittally.

Josh noticed that his rescuer was big like a Hawaiian.

But he was obviously a mixture that included Asian and Caucasian.

*Hapahaole,** Josh thought.

Being half-white is common in Hawaii. Since he had lived in the islands, Josh had taken special pride in trying to identify various nationalities by physical characteristics. It wasn't a very reliable method, but the new kid obviously had ancestors from several common Hawaiian races.

"I wanted to thank you for saving my life," Josh said quickly.

The boy anxiously scanned the area without acknowledging Josh's remark. Instead he said softly, "You guys better get out of here—fast!"

"Why?" Josh asked, his eyes darting around.

"Don't ask!" the boy replied in a hoarse warning whisper. "Just go! If they catch you here. . ." He left the sentence unfinished.

Josh hesitated, then said, "I'd like to be your friend. I'm Josh Ladd. He's Tank Catlett."

"Call me Duke Kahana. Now go!"

Josh glanced uncertainly at Tank, then shrugged. "Okay, Duke, if you insist, but—"

Suddenly, Tank tensed and cut in. "Listen!" he said. "Somebody's coming!"

Duke exploded, "Uh oh! Too late!"

Josh had a sickening feeling in his stomach as he turned toward the kiawe trees.

Chapter Three

TIDAL WAVE ALERT

Josh whispered tensely, "Tank, let's run into the water and paddle out on our. . ." He let his words trail off as an elderly man walked slowly out of the kiawe.*

"Whew!" Tank exclaimed in relief. "It's just an old kanaka!*"

The new arrival was obviously of Hawaiian descent. His wavy, gray hair had once been black. His brown skin was smooth, his nostrils were wide, and his face was serene. He weighed around three hundred pounds and stood close to six feet six inches tall. His full-length jeans were old, and he wore no shoes, shirt or hat.

Josh was also relieved to see the old Hawaiian instead of the two muscle men who had taken his videotape cassette.

"That's Kekoa!" Duke said quietly. "You guys are lucky it wasn't Barrel or Ox."

Josh realized Duke meant the barrel-shaped muscle man and the haole* with the chauffeur's cap. The nicknames suited them.

Duke added, "So get out of here while you can!" He picked up his surfboard and ran toward the water.

"Wait!" Josh called. "I want to—"

Tank interrupted by grabbing Josh's arm and hissing in his ear, "Don't yell! Those two muscle men might hear!"

"Sorry," Josh answered softly, glancing around anxiously. There was nobody else in sight except the old man. He came toward the boys steadily without giving any sign he'd heard or seen them.

"Must have poor eyesight," Tank muttered, "or else he's in another world."

Josh raised his voice. "Hi!"

The old man stopped in surprise. His sad, brown eyes swept the two boys. "Aloha!*" he replied. Then he walked on across the sand until he was about three feet away. "I'm looking for my grandson," he said. "Have you seen him?"

Josh had expected the old man to speak Pidgin English. Instead, his speech had a faintly Oriental flavor. Josh frowned, then pointed to the surf where Duke was paddling away. "You mean him?"

The gray-haired man shook his head. "That's not my grandson. That's Duke, the wild one. My grandson is called Akamu*—Adam in English. The tsunami* took him away, but the kahuna* told me the sea would bring him back. So I come every day and wait."

Josh and Tank exchanged glances. They had lived long enough in the islands to know that *tsunami* means "harbor wave" in Japanese. But in Hawaii, it's used to mean "tidal wave." Tidal waves hit the Hawaiian Islands about every three years, but there hadn't been one since Josh and Tank arrived in Honolulu.

To Josh, the old man's remark suggested he wasn't quite right mentally. Josh asked cautiously, "You mean you come here all the time even though it's a kapu* beach?"

"Yes. They don't try to stop me."

"They?" Josh asked, looking around for the men Duke had called Barrel and Ox.

The kanaka ignored Josh's question. "I am called Kekoa."

Josh nodded. "Yes, Duke told us. I'm Josh Ladd, and this is my best friend, Tank Catlett."

Kekoa extended his right hand and shook both boys' hands in turn. "Josh. Tank. My name means 'the courageous one' in English. Now you boys must excuse me, for it's time I was watching out to sea. This may be the day the tsunami returns my grandson to me."

Kekoa walked slowly toward the sparse shade of the twin coconut trees. The heavy nuts had been removed so they wouldn't fall on somebody's head.

Tank discreetly tapped his forehead with a forefinger and said, "He's pupule!*"

Josh nodded slightly, but his eyes followed Kekoa. "Let's go talk to him about Duke," he said thoughtfully.

"You crazy, too? Let's get out of here before those muscle men catch us!"

Reluctantly, Josh nodded. He glanced seaward just as

Duke caught a wave. At once, he seemed to become an extension of the hurtling board. He rode relaxed, yet with the poise and grace of a dancer, flowing from one motion to another. His arms moved rhythmically in harmony with his shifting legs.

"Wow!" Josh cried. "He's terrific! I've never seen anyone like him!"

"If we don't get out of here," Tank whispered hoarsely, glancing around, "neither of us may see *anything* again."

Josh took one final look at the distant Duke on the water. He shot back and forth along a curling wave, riding inside the half-closed mass of blue green water that threatened vainly to crash down on him.

"Magnificent!" Josh murmured, starting toward the kiawe. For a change, Tank was ahead, almost running.

Suddenly, Tank stopped and said, "Oops! It's them!"

The same two rough-looking men from the limo were leaving the kiawe trees at the edge of the beach. They bore down menacingly on the boys as Josh looked desperately for a way of escape.

The one Duke had called Barrel had heavily muscled, hairy legs. He wore walking shorts and leather sandals without socks. "Hey, you haole boys!" he growled. "You no read da sign? Dis beach kapu!"

"He doesn't recognize us yet!" Tank whispered.

"He will when they get closer! Grab your board and let's run into the water! Paddle out fast!"

"What if they've got guns?"

"Well, we can't stay and find out! Ready?"

Ox, the haole man with the chauffeur's cap, suddenly yelled, "Hey! It's them again!"

"Run!" Josh cried, snatching up his board and turning toward the sea.

"I'm running! Don't get in my way!" Tank exclaimed.

The boys sprinted across the white sand with the sound of the two men running behind and yelling "Stop!" in their ears.

Josh and Tank paddled furiously well out into the cove. With a rapidly beating heart, Josh finally risked twisting his head to look back at the two men. They stood at the water's edge, waving their fists and cursing.

Josh sighed with relief and turned to grin at his friend. "It's okay! They don't have weapons, and they can't follow us without boards."

"No come back!" one of the men shouted as a final threat. Josh recognized Barrel's Pidgin English.

"He doesn't need to worry," Tank muttered. "We're never coming back here!" He eased off on his paddling and looked at Josh. "What do you suppose is going on?"

"I don't know. I'm just glad to get away!" Josh turned to view the ocean, thinking maybe they could paddle out to talk to Duke, but he was too far out. *Some other time,* Josh thought.

The friends paddled their boards beyond the black volcanic wall and turned to their right. Then they caught waves and landed on Waikiki Beach* with its acres of white-skinned malihinis.* Josh and Tank picked their way through the brightly colored carpet of umbrellas, aloha shirts* and muumuus.* They emerged on Kalakaua* Avenue, crossed it, and headed up the street toward home.

Josh shifted his surfboard under his left arm. "I can't figure it out," he said. "I mean, what's going on with that kid—Duke—and those two men who chased us off? And why didn't they run the old kanaka away, too?"

"Maybe they're as pupule as—what's his name? Kekoa?—only in a different way."

"I feel sorry for him. He seems like a really nice guy, but sad. Of course, I can understand that, if a tidal wave really took his grandson's life. But believing the medicine man's claims that the sea will give the boy back—that's wild."

"Maybe the shock of losing his grandson made him lose his mind."

"I suppose that's possible. The two men could figure that Kekoa's off his rocker but harmless. Anyway, it's now obvious that those other men go wherever Duke goes. But why?"

Tank shrugged. "It's a mystery to me."

"If they're bodyguards, why does Duke need protection? Boy! If I could just talk to him!"

"You heard what those men said! Keep away from him or else!"

"Yeah, I know. Well, if we can't talk to him, maybe the old Hawaiian can tell us something."

"Forget it, Josh! I'm never going back there!"

"Maybe we won't have to do that. Kekoa must live around there. Duke might, too. Anyway, we could just wait near the fence and see if Kekoa comes along."

Tank grinned. "You don't think that big man squeezed through that little hole in the fence like us, do you?"

"No, I suppose—listen! What's that?"

Both boys stopped dead still. A wailing sound started and built rapidly to full, mournful and steady intensity. It seemed to come from every direction.

"It's nothing," Tank said. "They're just testing the tidal wave alert. The city does it on the first of every month."

"This is the twenty-seventh!" Josh exclaimed with sudden concern. "That must mean there's a real tidal wave alert!"

The boys glanced around. To both their right and left, several small objects resembling round birdhouses with tiny roofs rested on high metal poles. The terrible wailing sound continued pouring from the sirens.

Visitors on the street (they're never called tourists in Hawaii) seemed confused, not knowing the sirens' meaning. A few drivers pulled their cars to the curb and stopped as though expecting ambulances or police cars to pass. Other drivers kept moving down the street, apparently unconcerned.

Tank recalled, "Roger told me once that a thirty-five-foot tidal wave hit Hilo* on the Big Island, and sixty-one people drowned."

Josh gave a low whistle. "That's a wave taller than a three-story building! Come on! Let's get home!"

As the boys ran up toward Diamond Head, Tank puffed, "Roger also said another wave nearly sixty feet high hit the Big Island and left more than 150 dead! That'd be a wave nearly as high as a six-story building!"

"What tidal wave damage has there been here on Oahu?*"

"I don't know. Guess I just remember the most scary stories."

"Scary?" The word exploded from Josh's mouth. "Remember what the old Hawaiian said? 'This may be the day the tsunami returns my grandson to me.' Nah! That's crazy!" Still, Josh felt the short hairs on the back of his neck stand on end at the strange thought.

Breathing hard and tiring fast, the boys turned right on-to a dead-end street. Be-still trees* and twenty-foot-tall oleanders* grew on the left side, with Diamond Head just beyond. It rose massively in the clear Hawaiian sky like an ancient castle. Houses and apartments were on the right. Usually kids were playing in the street, but now there wasn't a single one.

"They must all be inside listening to the news," Josh guessed.

Tank pointed and said, "Hey! There's Manuel!"

Manuel Souza was considered very akamai* because he consistently made top grades in school. He stood on the front porch of his family's board and batten house.

It was built high off the ground to discourage termites from tunneling up through the dirt and destroying the wooden home from inside. The corrugated tin roof was rusted from seasonal rains. Banana trees were mixed with plumeria* shrubs in the front yard.

"Hi!" Manuel called. He brushed dark, wavy hair back from where the trade winds had blown it onto his olive-skinned forehead. "You malihinis are running as if this were your first tidal wave alert!"

"It is!" the two friends replied together, hurrying through a flock of mynah birds.* They hopped out of the way but didn't fly.

Josh stopped to catch his breath. "Where's everybody?"

Thirteen-year-old Manuel jerked a thumb toward twin concrete-block apartment buildings at the end of the street. "I saw both your families heading up the outside stairs to Roger's apartment. That's the highest and safest point around here, unless you climb Diamond Head."

"Why aren't you there, too?" Tank puffed.

Manuel shrugged. "I've been through too many false alarms. Besides, no tidal wave's ever come up this high that I know about. My folks think we're safe here. Well, my mom's calling. Gotta go." He waved, turned, opened the screen door, and disappeared into the house.

In another couple of minutes, Josh and Tank neared the farthest apartment building. Tank lived on the first floor, Josh on the second, and Roger Okamoto on the top floor.

Nathan, Josh's ten-year-old brother, shrieked from the

Okamotos' lanai* railing, "Here they come!"

Josh and Tank glanced up to see the small lanai filling with anxious family members and friends. Besides Nathan, Josh saw his mother; older sister, Tiffany; and Grandma Ladd. Tank's mother and older sister, Marsha, were also there, plus Roger and his mother. The three fathers were away at work. Josh saw his grandmother's lips moving. He guessed she was saying a thankful prayer that the boys were safe.

Nathan shouted down, "There's been an earthquake in Japan, and a tidal wave's coming this way! You guys better get up here before the wave drowns you!"

Josh and Tank eased their surfboards over the railing onto the lanai at the Catletts' apartment, then hurriedly climbed the stairs. They kicked their sandals off and left them outside the Okamotos' apartment door in the traditional Oriental custom.

Josh's family rushed up, anxious to know where he had been. Tank's mother and sister did the same.

"We were at Waikiki when the sirens started," Josh explained. He didn't feel this was the time to mention their experiences at Hidden Cove. "Now tell us about this tidal wave."

Mrs. Okamoto called from inside the apartment, "Another news bulletin!" She was short, with closely cropped black hair. Hurrying across the reed mat rug in straw slippers that squeaked with every step, she turned up the volume on the TV.

The boys and their families crowded into the small apartment. Josh caught the familiar sight of Japanese Kabuki dolls,* shoji screens* and other Oriental decorations. A samurai warrior* doll stood guard on top of the television set.

A male telecaster said, "Civil authorities have confirmed that an earthquake registering 7.1 on the open-ended Richter Scale* hit near Hokkaido* in the southern Kurils* off Japan earlier this morning. It has also been confirmed that the quake generated a tidal wave. It is now racing across the Pacific Ocean toward Hawaii at 450 miles an hour."

"Four hundred fifty—" Josh exclaimed, but everyone broke in, shushing him to silence.

The announcer continued, "The governor and other civil authorities are moving to a command post inside Diamond Head. As soon as it's known when the wave will hit these islands, we'll bring you word."

It took the excited and anxious Ladd and Catlett families some time to fill Josh and Tank in on what they'd heard so far. All three wives had talked to their husbands at work and knew they were safe in high-rise buildings.

Josh said, "I guess all we can do now is wait until the wave strikes here, huh?"

When the others agreed, Josh turned to Roger and whispered, "We need to talk to you!"

Roger was a slender, third-generation Japanese-American with very black hair that stuck straight out over his ears. He led the way down the hall to his bedroom. Roger motioned Josh and Tank to seats while he closed the door.

Briefly, Josh and Tank told him about their experiences at Hidden Cove.

Roger's eyes widened. "Now you two have done it!" he exclaimed. "You're in really big trouble!"

A PIECE OF THE PUZZLE

J osh leaned forward from the lower bunk bed where he was sitting in Roger's room. "Why are we in really big trouble?" he asked.

"Ask Manuel," Roger replied. "He knows more about that than I do."

"We can't leave here until the tidal wave alert's over," Josh protested.

Roger nodded. "Yeah. And you can't call, because the phone's in the living room, where everyone's listening to the news."

Josh agreed. "We don't want to upset our parents when we don't really know what this is all about. So, Roger, you tell us what you know, and we'll talk to Manuel later."

"Well," Roger began, looking from Josh to Tank, "for starters, his name's not Duke Kahana."

"It isn't?" Tank said.

"No. Duke's a very strange guy. He has no friends and won't make any. But once Manuel and I were waiting for a wave off Waikiki,* and Duke was nearby. We got to talk to him for a minute before he surfed away. He said his real name didn't matter, that he called himself after Duke Kahanamoku.*"

Josh nodded. Everybody knew about the native Hawaiian 1912 and 1920 Olympic champion who had introduced surfing to the world.

"Duke seems like a really nice guy," Roger continued, "but he's a loner and very quiet. I've never seen him talking to anybody more than a couple of minutes, and that was only way out in the surf. He doesn't even have a surfing buddy. But I had a funny feeling he was ashamed about something, especially when he wouldn't tell us where he lived or even where he came from."

Josh was surprised. "He's not from around here? The way he surfs, I thought he was a kamaaina.*"

"Maybe he is, but Duke won't say," Roger explained. "He never said anything about his family. He just said that surfing's all he ever wants to do, and that someday he'd like to ride a tidal wave."

"What?" Tank exclaimed.

Roger nodded. "That's not uncommon. Every time there's a tidal wave alert, some hotdog surfer announces he's going to wait offshore, then ride it in. It's especially not surprising about Duke. All of us who've seen him surf the big waves on the north shore think he takes too many risks. It's sort of like he doesn't care if he gets hurt or dies. That's why we call him 'the wild surfer.' "

While Josh frowned in thoughtful silence, Tank asked

Roger, "What do you know about Kekoa?"

"He's pupule!* His grandson disappeared about twelve, thirteen years ago. Manuel once looked through old newspaper files and found out the boy really was lost in a tidal wave. He was the only relative the old man had. I guess that made Kekoa go off into a world of his own."

"I thought you and Manuel didn't go down to Hidden Cove," Tank said.

"We don't. But Kekoa often comes to Waikiki Beach and watches from there." Roger shook his head. "Hidden Cove is a kapu* area. You'd be smart to never go there again. Above all, don't talk to Duke, because those two men—bodyguards or whatever they are—are always near him, except when he's surfing."

Josh's eyebrows shot up as a thought hit him, but Roger continued his explanation. "We heard about some guys who went to Hidden Cove, but those two men broke their boards and ran them off. We also heard that some guys went there and disappeared."

"Oh? Who?" Josh asked.

"Nobody we knew."

"Wasn't it in the papers?"

"Guess not."

"Then how do you know it's true?" Josh challenged.

"I don't," Roger said with a shrug, "but I believe it. I don't want to scare you two, but those men have seen you around Duke too often to just forget it. I'll bet they're already watching for you."

Josh wanted to know more, but his sister knocked on the bedroom door and called through it, "The first waves have hit Kauai,* so they'll be here soon."

Roger opened the door. "Soon as this alert is over, you'd better talk to Manuel," he warned.

"We will," Josh assured him.

In the Okamoto living room, the boys listened to the newscaster. "The neighboring island of Kauai recorded two fast waves, but they were only about a foot high. No damage was reported. Authorities say Oahu* can expect the first wave in fifteen minutes."

"That's us!" Josh's little brother exclaimed.

The newscaster continued, "Meanwhile, we have a tsunami* expert to explain what causes these often-destructive waves."

The scientist explained that a tidal wave is actually a series of long waves generated by a disturbance on the ocean floor, like an earthquake. A ship on the ocean might not even feel the wave pass. A tsunami does its damage in shallow water.

The announcer thanked the expert, then added, "Authorities have asked us to remind viewers that the trouble with these tidal wave alerts is that sometimes Hawaii has a couple in a short time, like a month apart. If there's no damage, as now appears likely in this situation, people get complacent. They don't take proper precautions. So when a dangerous wave does hit, people die."

Josh wasn't really listening. His mind jumped to the

mystery of Duke Kahana. *Is Roger right?* he wondered. *Maybe the two muscle men* will *be looking for Tank and me. But why?*

Fifteen minutes later, the television announcer reported, "Six waves from the tsunami have hit Oahu. The sixth was the largest, but all were so small they were barely noticeable. No damage has been reported. It's expected the 'all clear' will sound soon."

The moment that happened, Josh, Tank and Roger ran down the street to Manuel's house. He told his mother he was going walking with the boys. Then they all headed for the nearby main street leading to Waikiki.

"Tell us what you know about Duke Kahana," Josh urged Manuel.

Before Manuel could answer, Tank grabbed Josh's arm. "Look!" he said. "There goes that same limo!" He pointed toward the main street as the long, black vehicle moved slowly into the intersection, heading downhill toward Waikiki.

"You're right," Josh said. "They might be looking for us. Quick! Let's hide!"

Josh led the other three boys into a thick shelter of flowering red oleanders. They peered out warily at the stretch limo.

Josh felt his heart leap in concern. The windshield wasn't darkened like the other windows, so Josh had a quick glimpse of the driver. Josh couldn't be sure, but it looked like the big haole* Duke had called Ox.

A minute later Josh said, "Probably just coincidence. Come on. They've had time to get far enough down the street that they can't see us."

At the corner, the boys peered out cautiously from behind a plumeria fragrant with pale white and yellow blossoms. The limo turned off toward Honolulu. The four boys started down the street toward Waikiki.

Manuel began to tell what he knew about Duke. "A few days ago, I was at the library using some microfilm of old newspapers to research the Menehune* Competition. I'd been thinking about entering this year, and I wanted to see who I might be up against."

The annual surfing contest was held in age groups, starting with three-year-olds. The four friends were all either twelve or thirteen, the oldest group in the competition.

"I read something strange," Manuel continued. "Last year, Duke was ahead in our division and seemed certain to win. But he apparently blew it deliberately in the last heat so another kid would win."

Tank frowned. "Why would he do that?"

"Nobody knows, and Duke denied he did it on purpose, but not everyone believed him."

"That sounds to me as if he's a really good guy," Roger said. "I mean, helping another kid to win when Duke could have done that himself. But I'd like to know why, too."

Josh snapped his fingers. "Hmm. How about this for

a reason? The winner would have his picture in the paper and probably on television. Maybe Duke didn't want that. Maybe he doesn't want anybody to see him who might know his real identity."

An older teenage boy with long, untidy hair and wearing only dirty cutoffs came whizzing by on a skateboard. He stopped abruptly, flipped the board up, and caught it neatly in his right hand.

He glanced around before barely whispering to the four boys, "Buds?"

Josh frowned. "What's that?"

"Pakalolo,* you mainland haole!" the teenager muttered with scorn in his voice. "You want some?"

Manuel gave the boy a shove. "Get outta here!"

"Yeah!" Roger added, also shoving the boy. "Take your pakalolo someplace else!"

"Suit yourself," the skateboarder said as he zoomed on down the street.

Manuel looked at Josh and explained, "Pakalolo— that's what the locals call marijuana—is grown throughout these islands, even though it's illegal."

"I've heard it called pot and grass, but not buds," Josh replied.

"Buds is a word used by dopers for what they consider to be the best pot," Manuel said.

Josh had lost interest in the subject. He started to ask Manuel more about Duke, but Manuel spoke first.

"They say that marijuana's this state's biggest unofficial

cash crop. Of course, nobody talks about that out loud. But I heard pakalolo's worth more each year than sugarcane, pineapple, the military or even tourism."

"You're kidding!" Josh said.

"Wish I were," Manuel answered. "The police have tried to stop it, of course. They think the head guy in the business is a man named Richard Chong."

"I've heard of him," Tank said. "Isn't he supposed to be the godfather of crime in the islands?"

Manuel nodded and said, "Yes, but nobody can prove it. The police have arrested Chong several times but always had to let him go for lack of evidence."

Tank touched Josh's arm. "Look!"

The black limousine pulled out of a side street about a block away. It eased to a stop at the curb just as the long-haired teenager pulled up on his skateboard.

"What's going on?" Tank asked.

The four boys watched as the teenager stopped, carried his board to the curb, and stuck his free hand toward a darkened back window. It slid down, and a man's arm in a light blue suit coat reached out.

The hand was withdrawn, the window slid up, and the teenager returned to the sidewalk. He placed his right foot on the skateboard and disappeared down a side street. The limo drove on toward Waikiki.

"They exchanged something," Roger observed. "Probably money for dope."

Josh said thoughtfully, "There's a connection between

the limo and that pakalolo dealer. Hmm. I wonder. . ."

"What?" Tank asked as Josh let his thought trail off.

"I've got to talk to Duke to be sure."

"Why?" Tank asked.

"Because I think I've just found a piece of the puzzle. But I need more information, so I've got to talk to Duke—and Kekoa, if I get the chance."

"Oh, Josh!" Tank moaned. "You thanked Duke for saving your life, and we both got away from those two muscle men alive. Forget them!"

"Wish I could. But I liked Duke. I've got a hunch he needs somebody to be a real friend. Maybe Kekoa does, too."

"Sure," Tank said sarcastically, "there's lots of good reasons for being friends with a guy protected by bodyguards who threaten to hurt you! And everybody should be friends with an old man who's off his rocker!"

Josh took a slow, deep breath, looking at the three other boys thoughtfully before replying. "Duke saved my life. I owe him something."

"You thanked him. That's enough!" Tank protested. "Let Kekoa be his friend!"

Josh shook his head. "The two of them have had plenty of time to do that, but from what we saw, they go their separate ways. So it's obviously not working. They're sort of like two ships traveling in the same waters but without any communication between them."

Tank tried another approach. "Then let the bodyguards

be his friends."

"I don't think those two men are his bodyguards."

"You don't?" The startled chorus came from all three boys.

"No, I don't. I'm not sure why they're always around— maybe to keep other people away, like us. Anyway, I think Duke's in some kind of trouble and could use a friend. After what he did for me, I at least owe him enough to try talking to him. And if I can do that, maybe I can get some answers."

"You'll more likely get hurt," Tank said, "maybe even disappear like those people Roger mentioned."

"I think those are just stories without any truth in them. Anyway, guys, I've thought of a way to talk to Duke safely."

"How's that?" Tank asked.

"Roger said the only time those two men aren't around is when Duke's surfing. So I'll watch for him, and when I see him out waiting for a wave, I'll paddle out and talk to him."

Manuel asked, "What if those two men see you first, while you're still on shore?"

"I'll watch from Waikiki Beach. Those guys won't bother me with thousands of people around."

Grudgingly, Tank nodded. "Yeah, that might work. But what if you don't see Duke surfing off Waikiki?"

"Then I'll try talking to Kekoa. Maybe he's only a little 'off' on the subject of his grandson. And if that doesn't work, I'll watch until I see where either Duke or Kekoa lives. Maybe I can talk to them alone that way. Besides, as Roger pointed out, maybe those men are already looking for me."

"For *us,* you mean," Tank blurted.

"Okay, for us. So wouldn't you rather take action than sit around helplessly waiting for something terrible to happen?"

"I guess so. But what if none of these ideas works?"

"Then I'm going back into Hidden Cove!"

"I should have known!" Tank sputtered. "I'll go with you to Waikiki, but not to Hidden Cove!"

"I hope you don't mind, Josh, but I really don't want to go near any kapu place," Roger said.

"Neither do I," Manuel added.

"I understand," Josh said. "It's okay. But I've got to try to find Duke, so I'll see you guys later. Come on, Tank."

Roger and Manuel waved good-bye and turned for home, while Josh and Tank headed toward the ocean—and straight into danger.

Chapter 5

WARNING
FROM A STRANGER

As they hurried downhill, Tank asked, "What's this piece of the puzzle you mentioned a minute ago?"

"Well, when I saw that long-haired doper on the skateboard dealing with somebody in the limo, it all seemed to tie together, although I don't know how."

"If you're thinking it was Duke's arm we saw hand that teenager something, you're wrong. That arm was in a nice suit. Couldn't have been Duke."

"I didn't think it was. But it made me wonder: What's a logical reason those two muscle men keep everybody but Kekoa away from Duke? Ox and Barrel, as Duke called them, probably figure the old Hawaiian's too spaced-out over his lost grandson to be any threat."

"Are you saying those men are guarding Duke?"

"No, I think maybe he's some kind of prisoner."

"A prisoner? Who in the world would do that?"

"The only person I can think of is the pakalolo* god-father, Richard Chong."

Tank stopped and stared at his friend. "But why would

he do that?"

Josh shook his head. "I don't know, but if I can talk to Duke, maybe I can get a clue."

"If you're right about Chong, we're nuts to get mixed up in this in any way! It's too dangerous!"

"If it hadn't been for Duke, I'd be dead. If he's in some kind of trouble, I've got to help him." Josh hesitated, then added, "But it's not right for you to risk your life in this. Maybe you'd better go on home."

"I'd sure like to! But, well, I guess it'll be okay to just look for Duke."

Josh smiled. "You mean you're hoping we don't find him?"

Tank grinned back. "That thought had crossed my mind."

The boys spent an hour searching the beach and gazing at surfers riding the waves. Then the friends walked toward Hidden Cove, hoping to see Duke on the sidewalk.

Finally Tank said, "He may be surfing so far out we can't recognize him. Or maybe he's surfing off Hidden Cove. Anyway, it looks hopeless. Why don't we give it up for today?"

"Not yet!" Josh insisted. "They've got to live along here somewhere, because Kekoa goes to Hidden Cove or Waikiki* every day, and Duke's been seen around here by Manuel and Roger."

"How are you going to find where they live? The only way to do that is to follow them home sometime, and we can't even find either of them."

Josh scratched his head thoughtfully. "We've overlooked another possibility."

"What's that?"

"They've got to eat. Let's head into downtown Waikiki and check the coffee shops and grocery stores. Maybe we'll run into them."

"More likely we'll run into those muscle men," Tank muttered under his breath. But when Josh turned toward downtown Waikiki, Tank swung in step beside him.

Their search was still fruitless even after they had walked as far as the International Market Place. This is a thriving visitors' area of shops and large carts on wheels that can be closed up at night. The boys saw the usual gaudy array of Hawaiian souvenirs, scenic photos, clothes and jewelry. There were also a few grocery stores and all kinds of eating places. But there was no sign of Duke.

Finally, Tank again suggested, "Let's give it up."

Josh leaned against the main trunk of an immense banyan* tree and considered the idea. As his eyes probed the traffic on Kalakaua* Avenue, he suddenly stiffened.

"There's the limo!" he cried. "See? Coming down the street a couple of blocks away! If Duke's not in the car with them, he's somewhere close by. Keep looking!"

"You look! I'm going to keep an eye on that limo so those two men don't get too close to us."

Josh and Tank eased toward the street, taking care to stay behind a crowd of Japanese visitors.

"There's Duke!" Josh exclaimed.

"Where?"

"Across the street! Wearing those same green trunks and carrying his surfboard! I don't want to point because those guys in the limo must be watching him, and I don't want to attract their attention."

"It's okay! I see him."

Duke emerged from between two old, small, frame buildings left over from before the modern high-rise condos and hotels had sprung up all around Waikiki Beach.

Josh and Tank followed a block behind as Duke made his way down the sidewalk nearer the ocean.

Josh turned to look back. "Here comes the limo!" he said.

Even from a distance, through the clear windshield, Josh recognized the chauffeur with the broken nose. The barrel-shaped man sat beside him. The darkened side windows prevented Josh from seeing if anyone was in the back seat.

Josh and Tank moved on slowly, staying deep in crowds of visitors with their colorful island clothing. Josh's eyes darted alternately from the limo behind to the boy in green trunks ahead.

Duke turned around and looked back. Josh guessed he was checking on the limo's whereabouts. For a second, Duke seemed to look across the street right at the two boys. Then he turned around and continued on his way.

"For a moment there, I thought he saw us," Tank

whispered.

"Maybe he did! He's starting to cross the street to this side!"

Josh felt his heart speed up at the thought that Duke might be waiting for them. That would surely bring Barrel leaping out of the limo to chase them away.

"Uh oh!" Tank exclaimed. "I think those men saw us!"

Josh turned to see the stretch limo brake sharply. Barrel jumped out of the front passenger door and darted across the busy street, ignoring squealing brakes and the angry honking of horns.

"Split up!" Josh cried. "Run back in the marketplace a little way with me, then you go left and I'll go right. Barrel can only follow one of us. The other should try to find Duke!"

"Won't do me any good to find him, because I don't know the questions you want to ask. I'll try to make Barrel chase me."

The boys hurried off the sidewalk into the marketplace again. "How'll you do that?" Josh asked.

"Maybe pretend to hurt my leg or something so Barrel will think I'm easier to catch."

"Just see that he doesn't!"

"Don't worry!"

Josh nodded. "Get ready to split." He swiveled his head and glanced to the right. "Hey! Where'd Duke go?"

Duke was nowhere in sight. Behind him, Josh heard startled cries from the crowd of visitors as Barrel roughly pushed his way through, closing in on Josh and Tank. "Duke can't have gone far," Josh said. "I'll try to find him! Keep an eye on Barrel! Okay, split up!"

Tank cut sharply away to the left. Josh veered to the right. He darted into an area packed with visitors swarming around open-front shops and handcarts.

Taking a quick look over his shoulder, Josh saw that Tank was hobbling along barely twenty feet in front of the onrushing pursuer. But even as Josh watched, Barrel turned away from Tank and pounded hard to the right.

Barrel's coming straight for me! Josh thought as he hurried down a narrow aisle between large handcarts. *Guess he figured out Tank's limping was faked. Now how am I going to get away so I can find Duke?*

Josh dashed behind a small shop with its entire front open to display a wild assortment of Hawaiian leisure clothes. Josh's arms were pumping hard as he ran. Suddenly, out of the corner of his eye, he saw a hand reach out fast. He started to dodge, but his left arm was seized. He was jerked behind the shop so hard he started to fall.

Ox! Josh's mind screamed as he tried to regain his balance and pull free. *He must've left the limo and—Duke!*

"Stop trying to jerk my arm off!" Duke chided, letting go of Josh. Duke's hands were empty, showing he had left his surfboard someplace. "I saw you and Tank following me. Split up, huh? Good thinking. You ready for us to outrun Barrel?"

"I've been trying!" Josh panted. He glanced around to see that the stout man had stopped and was turning quickly in various directions to see where his quarry had gone. Just then Duke's words sank in, and Josh swung back to face the other boy.

"Did you say, 'Ready for *us*'?" he asked.

"You want to talk to me, don't you? Then let's give Barrel some exercise. I do that sometimes just to make him earn his money. Let's lose him! Follow me!"

Duke turned and raced through the shops and carts.

Josh hesitated a moment to glance back at Barrel. Their eyes met for a second. "Stop, haole* boy!" the man yelled. He started running toward Josh on stubby legs that carried him faster than Josh would have guessed possible.

Whirling around and running after Duke, Josh called, "Wait for me!"

Josh ran hard, staying a couple of steps behind Duke. They dodged in and out among the small shops and large handcarts. Merchants and customers stared in startled surprise as the boys dashed past. Quickly they came to a large banyan tree in the middle of the little shops.

Duke slowed, looked over his shoulder, then stopped, panting hard. "We've lost him," he said. "Let's stop and catch our breath. You okay?"

Josh nodded, breathing hard and shooting anxious looks behind to make sure they were safe. Barrel was nowhere in sight.

Turning back to Duke, Josh asked in panting breaths,

"Who is he? What's going on?"

Duke grinned. "I don't know his real name, so I just call him Barrel because he looks like one—with legs. I don't know the chauffeur, either, so I just call him Ox, although I can think of other names that would do."

Josh nodded and glanced around for Tank. He wasn't anywhere in sight, either. From this part of the marketplace, it was impossible to see the street, the limo or the big haole driver.

"It's okay," Duke assured Josh. "Ox wouldn't just jump out and leave the car in the middle of the street to chase your friend, so he's safe."

"You guessed I wanted to talk to you?" Josh asked, breathing easier.

"Yep! Lots of other kids do, too, but they're always scared off by Ox and Barrel. I figured if you and your friend—what's his name? Tank?"

Josh nodded.

"I figured if you two wanted to risk talking that much, I'd see if we could get a chance. But I can tell you right now I can't answer all your questions."

Both boys fell into step, sauntering through the small shops and handcarts parallel to Kalakaua. Josh asked, "Can you at least tell me something about why those guys follow you and keep everyone away?"

"No, but believe me, I don't like it one little bit! I just want to lead my own life in my own way."

"What about your parents? Can't they make those guys

leave you alone?"

"They're dead. No living relatives except—oh! There's your friend."

Through the shops and handcarts, Josh glimpsed Tank. He was a hundred yards to the right, pressed against the side of a handcart that hadn't opened for business. Josh breathed a quick prayer of thanks and glanced around to make sure Barrel wasn't close by.

Then Josh and Duke headed toward Tank. Josh prompted, "You were saying you've got no living relatives except..."

"Except one." Duke's voice took on a hard, bitter edge. "But I don't want to talk about him."

"Him?"

Duke shook his head. "I told you—"

"Okay! Okay!" Josh interrupted. "I told Tank that I've got an idea there's some connection between you and Richard Chong, the pakalolo godfather."

Duke stopped instantly, glaring at Josh. "Do you know what you just said?"

"Well, I didn't mean you've done anything wrong—"

"If you want to be my friend," Duke broke in harshly, "you never mention that name again in front of me! Okay?"

"Okay." Josh nodded. "I just—"

"Forget it!"

They walked in strained silence until they were even with Tank. He still hadn't seen them. Josh glanced up and down the street but couldn't see Barrel or the limo.

"I'm sorry," Josh said at last. "I just want to be friends. I didn't mean to hurt your feelings."

Duke managed a smile. "I understand. I like your style, Josh. You and Tank don't scare easily. If you're willing to risk Ox and Barrel again, maybe you and Tank could go surfing with me sometime."

The invitation was so totally unexpected, especially in light of Duke's sharp words moments before, that Josh was surprised. "We'd love to! But your bodyguards— "

"They're not my bodyguards! They're more like my keepers, my jailers."

"Your jailers?"

"There's no time to explain, but I'd like to talk to someone who's not afraid to be my friend. Meet me tomorrow morning about ten outside the fence at Hidden Cove. I know a trick to keep Ox and Barrel away so they won't bother us. Will you come?"

"I'll be there!"

Josh and Tank were reunited without any sign of Barrel or the limo. They headed for home while Josh related what Duke had said.

As Josh finished, he heard a car slow and pull to the curb beside them. Both boys turned.

The black limo with Ox behind the wheel and Barrel in the front seat sat next to them. The darkened passenger-side rear window slid down noiselessly a couple of inches and stopped.

A man's voice commanded, "Don't run! I just want to talk!"

Josh hesitated, tensed to flee with Tank beside him. But Josh had a feeling Barrel and Ox would be out of the car quickly, chasing them down, if they tried running.

Josh tried to peer into the gloomy interior of the limo. He could make out only the outline of a man wearing an expensive straw hat.

The man leaned forward, the brim hiding his face. Josh caught the glitter of hard eyes through the small opening.

"You're Josh Ladd." The voice was soft and gentle, yet filled with menace. "Your blond-headed friend is Tank Catlett. I know all about both of you and your families."

Josh felt his heart speed up. He forced his voice to be calm. "Who are you?"

"Never mind who I am!" The man's voice was harsh, then instantly changed back. "You boys want a little friendly advice?" There was no edge of threat, yet it was there, sharp as a keen blade. It wasn't at all what Josh would have expected.

Without waiting for an answer, the voice continued in an almost-purring quality. "You've been warned before. Now I'm telling you. Don't ever again go near the kid who calls himself Duke!"

Josh swallowed hard as the man said in the same reasonable-sounding tone, "If you boys are foolish enough to risk your own lives, remember your families. You don't want anything to happen to them, do you?"

Josh and Tank shook their heads as the car window started to slide up silently.

The man added with deadly softness, "This is your final warning!"

Chapter Six

A MYSTERIOUS DISAPPEARANCE

When Josh got home, he promptly told his mother all that had happened. His sister and brother also listened closely, but Grandma Ladd was away at the nearby branch library, one of her favorite places.

As soon as Josh finished describing the final warning from the man in the hat, Mrs. Ladd said, "I'll phone your father first, then the police." She hurried to the kitchen wall phone.

"Will that man in the black car hurt us?" Nathan asked.

"I don't think so," Josh said, rumpling the ten-year-old's hair. "I think they're just trying to scare us."

Tiffany asked under her breath, "Josh, why do you always get yourself in trouble?"

"It's not my fault! Duke saved my life, and I was just trying to—"

"Children!" their mother chided from the phone. "Please! It's ringing." She impatiently patted her dark hair until her husband's office answered. "John Ladd, please," she said crisply. "His wife is calling. Please hurr—What? Oh! Thanks."

She hung up and explained to her children, "Your father's on the windward side of the island. He won't be where we can reach him by phone, so we'll just have to handle this problem ourselves. I'll call the police."

As Mary Ladd dialed again, fourteen-year-old Tiffany automatically assumed her big-sister role. "Nathan, you be very careful!" she warned. "Since you're the smallest, those men might pick on you!"

"Aw, Tif!" Nathan muttered angrily. "You treat me like I was a little kid. I can take care of myself!"

Tiffany, who was tall for her age, snapped, "You're the smallest kid in your class! And you're immature for your age! So listen—"

"I am not!" Nathan flared.

"Children!" their mother said firmly, clamping her hand over the mouthpiece. "Please!" She removed her hand and spoke into the phone. "Hello. I'd like to report a threat to my family."

About half an hour later, a plainclothes police officer arrived in an unmarked car. He glanced down at the sandals outside the Ladds' apartment door and began removing his shoes as Mrs. Ladd opened the screen door for him.

"Mrs. Ladd," he said, showing his badge and ID card, "I'm Sergeant Park, narcotics division."

"These are my children: Tiffany, Josh and Nathan. Please come in, Sergeant Park."

As the officer walked across the off-white rug in his stocking feet, Josh guessed the man was of Korean descent. His last name was common among Hawaii's many residents whose ancestors came from that Asian country.

The narcotics officer sat in the rattan occasional chair Mrs. Ladd indicated. He took out a notebook and a pen. "Mrs. Ladd," he said, "I was sent in answer to your call because you led the dispatcher to believe narcotics may be involved. Now, let me take your son's statement, please."

Josh told everything from the beginning to the "final warning" he'd received a short time before.

When Josh had finished, the officer closed his notebook. "The man in the hat who spoke to you from the limo sounds like Richard Chong," he concluded. "We believe he's the boss of illegal drugs in these islands. We've never been able to get enough evidence to convict him, but with your help, Josh, maybe we can."

Sergeant Park stood up and walked toward the door. "I want to consult with my superiors about setting up some surveillance. I'll be in touch tomorrow morning. In the meantime, please don't tell anyone who I am or why I was here—except your husband, of course, Mrs. Ladd."

"What about Tank?" Josh asked. "He was with me when we were threatened."

The officer shook his head. "The fewer people who know about this, the better. But our agents will protect your friend and his family, too."

Josh didn't like not telling Tank, even though he had been upset the last time they talked. However, Josh agreed with his mother, sister and brother to say nothing about the surveillance except to his dad and Grandma Ladd. They didn't want to worry her but felt that since she was living with them, she had to know.

After the officer had left, Nathan asked, "Does 'surveillance' mean there'll be guys in trench coats hiding behind the bushes?"

His mother explained, "It's whenever somebody is watched by another person, or even by hidden microphones and video cameras."

"Oh, yeah!" Nathan cried. "I've seen that on TV! Sergeant Park is a real narc! And he's going to spy on us with 'bugs' and other secret things!"

Tiffany rolled her eyes in big-sister disgust. "Their surveillance will be on all the people involved, not just us! And we'll be watched only for our protection. Same with Tank."

Mrs. Ladd said gently, "Nathan, Sergeant Park is a narcotics agent. Please don't call him a narc. Just go on about your regular routines, but remember to say nothing about this."

"Can I go outside and play?" Nathan asked.

"I suppose that's safe," his mother answered. "But stay close. Tiffany, you and Josh please help watch him."

"Aw, Mom!" Nathan growled. "Just because I'm the youngest doesn't mean you have to treat me like a baby.

I can take care of myself! Besides, if I wanted, I could get away from Tif or Josh or anybody!"

He stormed out through the sliding screen door without stopping to pick up his zoris.* Then he ran barefoot down the outside stairs to the parking lot behind the apartments.

"What's the matter with him, Mom?" Tiffany asked.

"Maybe he's just tired of being the baby in the family. I remember feeling that way myself when I was about his age. I was the youngest of six, so it seemed worse."

The rest of the afternoon, Josh was restless. He was bothered by not being allowed to tell Tank about the narcotics agent. To avoid the tension of being with Tank and yet having to keep silent, Josh stayed in his room. Through the open, louvered window, he watched his little brother playing with other neighborhood kids.

After a while, Josh told Tiffany he wanted to read, and she agreed to watch Nathan. But Josh couldn't keep his mind on his book. He kept thinking about Duke and the men who had threatened him. *Would they really do something to me or my family?* Josh asked himself over and over.

Dusk was approaching when Josh heard his father arrive home. As the boy hurried down the hallway to tell his father what had happened, Josh heard Grandma Ladd's voice. He guessed his father had seen her walking home from the library and picked her up.

"Hey, Dad!" Tiffany called before Josh could get to the

living room. "Guess what kind of trouble Josh got into today."

Josh muttered to himself, "Sometimes big sisters can be such a pain!" Then he dashed up to his father, saying, "Let me tell it, Tiffany!"

While his parents, grandmother and sister listened, Josh repeated for his father all that had happened. Tiffany frequently interrupted to add information about what Sergeant Park had said, especially about the surveillance possibility.

"I promised Duke I'd meet him tomorrow morning," Josh concluded, "so what should I do, Dad?"

Before he could reply, Josh's mother looked up anxiously. "Where's Nathan?" she asked.

"He's playing downstairs," Tiffany answered.

Mrs. Ladd hurried to the lanai* and leaned over the railing. "Nathan!" she called.

There was no answer.

Josh led the rush to the lanai to glance around and ask the few kids playing below, "Have you seen Nathan?"

"Not for a while," one little girl yelled back through cupped hands. "The last I saw, he was heading that way." She pointed toward the main street that led to Waikiki.*

"Oh, no!" Mrs. Ladd exclaimed, turning anguished eyes to Tiffany and Josh. "I thought you two were watching him!"

Josh was tempted to say, "I did for a while, then Tiffany said she would," but he glanced at his sister's stricken face and decided not to. Instead, he ran for his zoris at the door. "He's probably down at Manuel's," he suggested.

That wasn't logical, since Manuel had no younger brothers or sisters, but Josh didn't want to alarm his mother any further. He slap-slapped down the concrete stairs while his father gave instructions for the other family members to search in various places.

Half an hour passed, and nobody had found a sign of Nathan. Neighbors were alerted as darkness fell. Josh and his family honored the narcotics officer's request that they not say anything about his visit.

Since Tank didn't know about that, he told friends and neighbors about the warning Josh and he had been given from the man in the hat.

Roger's and Tank's fathers took flashlights and hurried up the side of Diamond Head to search the tunnels inside the ancient volcano. They returned some time later without finding Nathan.

Roger's and Tank's mothers joined the Ladd family in knocking on every door in the apartment buildings. Again, there was no sign of the boy.

Manuel soon reported that he'd been to every house in the neighborhood, without success, except for one: "The lady on the corner said she saw Nathan walking down toward Waikiki by himself."

Josh saw the terrified look on his mother's face. "Oh, Josh!" she exclaimed. "Those terrible men must have seen him there and kidnapped him!" She turned to call the police, but her husband beat her to it.

The night was black by the time the police joined in the search. Dinner was forgotten as the Ladd family broadened the areas of exploration. Grandma Ladd stayed by the telephone.

Josh was upset, so a natural tendency was to strike out—to blame somebody. He turned from rechecking possible hiding places in the dense bamboo separating the apartments from Diamond Head's slope and glared at his sister.

"You shouldn't have let him out of your sight, Tif!" he said.

He wasn't prepared for her reply. "I know it!" she wailed, tears filling her eyes. "I watched him until Dad and Grandma got home! Then I wanted to tell Dad about the threat and the policeman and everything, so I forgot!"

Mr. Ladd, who was getting into his station wagon to drive around the neighborhood again, spoke sternly. "Tiffany! Joshua! There's no point in blaming yourselves! Save your energy for the search. I'll be back shortly."

Josh ran across the parking lot, his zoris slapping noisily on the asphalt. "Let me ride with you!" he pleaded. "Please!"

"I'd rather you stayed here, Son." His father lowered his voice as Josh stood outside the open driver's window. "If—if your brother was kidnapped, there's a good likelihood a phone call may come from the people who took him. Please stay with your grandmother until I get back."

Josh obeyed, jumping every time the phone rang. He listened, holding his breath, when his grandmother answered. But it was always a friend or neighbor reporting no sign of Nathan in an assigned search area, or someone with a suggestion about where else to look.

Josh felt sick inside. He told himself fiercely, *It's really my fault! I got us all into this! Can't blame Tif, either. I should've helped keep an eye on Nathan after Dad got home.*

When Mr. Ladd returned from another fruitless search, he called his family together in their apartment. "I know you've all been praying individually," he said, "but now I'd like us to join together as a family to pray for Nathan's safe return."

Josh's father cleared his throat and started to pray just as the phone rang. Josh was nearest, so he snatched it up. "Hello?"

"Josh!" The voice was small and frightened in his ear.

"Nathan! Where are you? Are you all right?"

Before his brother could answer, their father grabbed the receiver. He started to speak, but Josh could hear his little brother's voice talking, although the words were unclear.

"You stay put, Nathan!" John Ladd said. "I'll be there in two minutes!" He slammed the receiver down and cried joyfully to his family, "He's all right! He got locked in the library when it closed for the night."

A wild hubbub exploded around him as Mr. Ladd phoned the police to report what had happened. He added into the receiver, "I'm on my way there. Can you have someone with a key meet us there right away? Thanks!" Questions poured out of Josh and his family as all except Grandma rushed downstairs to the station wagon. When they arrived at the branch library, two uniformed policemen were already waiting. Their flashlights on the front door showed the face of a very frightened young boy pressed against the glass on the other side.

It took another half hour for someone from the library to arrive with a key. When the door was opened and Nathan had been thoroughly welcomed with glad cries and hugs, the boy told what had happened.

"Tiffany and Josh said they could watch me because everybody always treats me like a baby. Remember I said I could take care of myself, and if I wanted I could get away from Tif or Josh or anybody? Well, I decided to prove it. So when I saw Josh and Tif weren't watching me, I walked away. I went down to the library because Grandma was there, but I couldn't find her.

"So I started home, but then I saw a big, black car stop outside. I recognized the two men Josh told about, so I ran back into the library and hid in a closet. I was so scared they were looking for me that I stayed there a long time.

"When it got real quiet and I thought it was safe, I opened the closet door, and the library was dark.

Everybody had gone home! I found a pay phone, but I didn't have any money. Finally, I thought about the librarian's phone behind her desk, so I used that."

The Ladd family didn't go to sleep for a long time that night. It was nearly midnight before friends and neighbors had finally gone and the phone had stopped ringing.

At breakfast the next morning, Josh brought up an unresolved problem he faced. "Dad, I told Duke I'd meet him this morning, and I don't want to break my word. What should I do?"

"Son, I appreciate your obligation to that boy you call Duke, but his friendship isn't worth risking—"

"But he saved my life!" Josh interrupted.

Mr. Ladd speared a slice of papaya with his fork before answering. "We must wait for Sergeant Park to call about whether he's going to set up a surveillance that would protect you."

"Could I at least send Duke a message through the old Hawaiian man Kekoa?"

"Hmm. All right, if you can do that without doing anything that might cause that man in the limo to carry out his threat."

"Thanks, Dad!" Josh pushed his chair back and asked to be excused just as the phone rang. His father answered it, then motioned for Josh to wait.

After his father hung up, he looked at Josh. "That was Sergeant Park," he said. "His department is going ahead with the surveillance. For now, he wants you to stay away from Duke, but it's okay to talk to the old Hawaiian man. Sergeant Park wants you to act as though you didn't know anything about the surveillance. And you mustn't tell anyone, not even Tank!"

Josh started downstairs with mixed feelings of hope and fear about what might happen next.

Chapter Seven

THE CHASE

Josh intended to go alone to talk to the old Hawaiian, but Tank was waiting downstairs.

"You still going to meet Duke this morning?" he asked.

Josh shook his head. "I'm going to ask Kekoa to tell Duke I can't come."

"I'll go with you."

"After the man in the hat threatened us yesterday, you said I'd have to go alone."

"I changed my mind after the scare we had last night with your kid brother, although it's still against my better judgment. I mean, suppose Ox and Barrel see you? They'll think you're trying to talk with Duke, and you know what that'll mean!"

"I've got no choice, Tank! But if Kekoa will give me some idea of what this is all about, maybe I can figure out a way to deal with it."

The boys left their surfboards at home and started walking. Tank asked, "All because Duke saved your life?"

"That, of course, but I also like both Duke and Kekoa.

I can't just walk away without trying to help."

Tank sighed. "Well, I'll probably regret this, but I'll stand guard. If I see those two muscle heads driving along, I'll give a signal so you and Kekoa can duck out of sight."

"Thanks!" Josh clapped his friend on the back.

The boys walked down from Diamond Head and stopped across the street from the invisible entrance to Hidden Cove. They looked around carefully as traffic moved up and down the street, but there was no sign of the limo or its occupants. The boys settled down to wait.

About half an hour later, Josh saw Kekoa coming down the sidewalk on the opposite side of the street, nearer the ocean. Josh stood up. "Let's hope he'll tell me something this time," he said. "Keep a sharp eye out for those men."

"I'll whistle three times if they show up."

Josh waited until the way was clear of cars, then dashed across the street and approached Kekoa. "Morning," Josh began. "Mind if I walk with you a little way?"

"It would delight this old man's heart to have your young presence."

As Josh fell in step, he said, "You know, I'm still surprised that you don't talk with more of a local accent. Fact is, I think you sound more Oriental than Hawaiian."

Kekoa smiled. "I had many Asian teachers when I was in school."

Josh glanced around. "Uh, would it be all right with you if we walked down a side street?"

"A prudent suggestion, Josh! There's no sense in possibly antagonizing those men who shadow Duke. Follow me!"

The old man turned right, away from Diamond Head. Josh turned back to see Tank settled against the base of a monkeypod tree.* He'd be hard to see by the approaching limo, but he could spot the car and give a signal with a minimum of exposure.

Josh and Kekoa walked a few steps while the boy tried to think of what he wanted to say. Finally, he decided on a roundabout advance.

"You born here on Oahu?*"

"No, on Molokai.*"

"When did you move here?"

"I thought about it when my son married and left Molokai. I had been a widower many years by then. When he and his wife had a baby, I decided I wanted to be near them, so I came here."

The old man's voice broke, and he stopped talking.

Josh didn't know what to say, so he walked in silence.

After a while, Kekoa added softly, "They said they didn't blame me for letting the tsunami* take the baby, but I blame myself. It was my fault. I was foolish, and the sea robbed me of my only grandson."

He looked at Josh through misty, brown eyes. "My son and his wife died in an auto accident about two years later. So I have nothing left until the sea brings my grandson back."

Josh ached for the old man, knowing his wait was in vain. Josh thought that perhaps Kekoa's guilt and pain would be too great to bear if he allowed himself to realize the truth, so he lived with a dream.

The boy moved the conversation closer to the reason he had come. "You look like a pure Hawaiian, but I understand there are almost none left."

"I'm half Hawaiian on my mother's side. My father was Portuguese, Japanese and Chinese. But I consider myself a real Hawaiian."

"You have brothers and sisters?"

"No, I'm an only child. My parents both died of the white man's disease—measles—when I was little. My tutu* raised me."

"Tutu?" Josh asked. "Doesn't that mean 'grandmother'?"

"Yes. Her husband was tutu makua.* He weighed 360 pounds and stood six foot seven. He was a stern man who was gone a lot, so Tutu raised me.

"Both were pure Hawaiians. My tutu weighed 320 pounds and stood six feet tall. She didn't like me to speak English to her when I was little.

"When I did, she would say, 'What 'at? What you talking?'"

Kekoa's eyes took on a faraway look. "She sometimes explained her life's philosophy in Pidgin English, like this:

"'God went give me one piece land.' She'd hold out

her hand toward the place where we lived. It was a weathered, board and batten house high off the ground. The roof was rusted tin such as you still see around here. My tutu would say, 'I plant taro* for poi.* I plant planty food for my son and moopunas*'—that's grandchildren—'to eat. I make my land green. Planty food, and dat's why.' "

Josh was touched. "She sounds like a wonderful person," he said.

"She was, but she said something that wasn't true. You see, she didn't own a piece of land. She had rented one for fifteen years."

"Then why did she say that God gave her a piece of land?"

"It was kind of a Hawaiian attitude, Josh. God—not people—owned all the land, and He gave her a piece of it to use."

"That's a nice philosophy." Josh hesitated, then asked, "The other day you mentioned the kahuna,* or Hawaiian priest. Does that mean you don't believe in God?"

Kekoa laughed. "Have you seen the stories in the newspapers when a new airplane or ship is christened or dedicated here? There's usually a kahuna officiating along with a pastor or a priest. We Hawaiians don't take any chances!"

Josh wanted to know about Duke before asking Kekoa to carry a message saying he couldn't meet with him. Before speaking again, though, he glanced back. He didn't know what a surveillance team would look like, but he assumed they were probably people in one of the several cars and vans parked along the street.

There was no sign of Tank, yet Josh was sure he could hear him if he gave the warning signal. Josh looked up at the old Hawaiian again.

"Can you tell me about Duke?" he said. "It's very important to me."

Kekoa cocked his head slightly to one side and studied the boy before answering. Finally he said, "You have been threatened?"

Josh thought quickly, nodded, and explained the warning from Ox and Barrel. He omitted the "final warning" from the limo and the planned surveillance.

"And you're still willing to risk coming here just for Duke's friendship?" Kekoa asked.

"Well, Duke saved my life. Besides, I like him, and I think he needs a friend. If he'd let me, I'd like to be a friend. So would Tank."

"Even with the threats?"

Josh nodded and added, "We'd like to be your friend, too, Kekoa."

"Mahalo,*" the old man said softly, then fell silent.

"Can't you please tell me something about Duke?" Josh asked again.

Kekoa didn't answer. He continued walking in silence, and Josh didn't speak, either. Josh lifted his eyes to a Hawaiian state flag flying on a pole. The Union Jack in the upper left corner symbolized Britain's historic role in the islands. The flag blew makai,* toward the sea.

Beyond the pole, over the ocean, a huge 747 airliner with the Japan Air Lines insignia eased past, heading for the Honolulu International Airport. Josh caught a whiff of the nearby ocean. This morning it had a faintly fishy odor, unlike the usual pineapple fragrance.

At length the old Hawaiian replied. "His real name is not Duke Kahana. I'm sure you suspected that."

"Yes."

"His mother was a famous island 'cosmopolitan' beauty of many racial mixtures."

"Was?" Josh asked. "Is she dead?"

"Yes. So is Duke's father."

Josh wondered where Duke lived, who cared for him, and so forth, but it wasn't the time to ask. "Go on," he urged.

"Duke's mother was the only daughter of—"

Kekoa broke off his sentence as three sharp whistles split the air.

Josh whirled around in alarm to face Diamond Head. It was dry and brown as an old boot. The boy dropped his eyes to where he'd left Tank, but he wasn't in sight.

"That's Tank's whistle!" Josh exclaimed. "That means the limo's coming with those muscle men!" Josh momentarily forgot about Sergeant Park's surveillance team.

"Follow me!" Kekoa bent his massive shoulders so he was about a quarter of the way doubled over. He hurried alongside a six-foot-high beefsteak hedge* of dark reddish leaves. He moved with surprising speed for such a big man.

Josh also bent forward so the hedge would hide him from the limo's occupants. He hurried after Kekoa, hardly noticing the sweet fragrance of nearby plumerias or seeing the banana and mango* trees that grew everywhere in subtropical profusion.

"I hear the limo coming closer!" Josh exclaimed.

"Keep moving, my bold, young friend!"

Josh obeyed, thinking, *Duke said he had a way of keeping those men away so he and I could meet today. Something must've gone wrong! And where's the surveillance team? Will they help if I get in trouble?*

Josh judged the sound meant the car was very close, as Kekoa stopped dead still in the shadow of a mango tree. Josh did the same, freezing every action except his breathing and eye movements.

The black stretch limo came even with the beefsteak hedge and then moved on slowly. Through the clear windshield, Josh saw Ox and Barrel in the front seat. The blackened side windows looked like giant eyes that betrayed nothing of who was behind them.

"They're passing," Josh whispered to Kekoa. "They didn't see us."

"Don't move until they're out of sight!"

Josh nodded and held himself perfectly still until the limo's large, boomerang-shaped trunk antenna had vanished.

"Whew!" the boy exclaimed with a relieved smile. "That was close!"

"They must have been watching from some distance back," Kekoa mused, "or they would not have known to turn down this street. So we had better part. Can you find your way back from here?"

"Yes, but what about you?"

"They won't bother me. You rejoin Tank and have a safe trip home."

"But you didn't get to finish telling me about Duke's family!"

"Some other time, perhaps."

"Wait! Will you please take a message to Duke? Tell him I'm sorry I can't meet him today as we planned. I'll explain later."

"I'll do it, my young friend. Listen! I heard a car door slam! They must've seen us!" Kekoa pointed. "See that alligator pear tree* over there? There's a path just beyond it that will take you back to the street."

"Thanks!" Josh said before dashing to the designated tree. He crouched there, glancing back to see that Kekoa had already vanished into the tangle of subtropical undergrowth.

Josh started running along the path, trying to make as little noise as possible. *Where's Tank?* he thought. *And Sergeant Park?*

As he neared the street, Josh thought, *Now if I can just find Tank before those guys in the limo...*

For a moment, Josh wondered if Ox or Barrel had caught Tank. Then he sighed with relief as he saw his friend in the shadow of the monkeypod tree. Josh started running silently toward him.

As he passed a large, fragrant plumeria, he heard Tank's warning yell: "Josh! Look out!"

The huge chauffeur exploded from behind the plumeria and grabbed for the boy. Josh slid to a stop and dodged aside. In the same instant, he whirled away and started running back toward the sea.

"Stop, kid!" Ox's voice from behind hit like a clap of thunder.

But Josh didn't stop. *Where's Barrel?* he wondered, dashing as fast as he could between a high, stone fence covered with lavender bougainvillea* blossoms on the left and a wrought iron fence on the right. He heard heavy footsteps gaining on him rapidly.

Suddenly, three feet ahead, the barrel-shaped man leaped out from behind a huge, flowering, red hibiscus.*

"Now we got you, kid!" he cried.

Josh tried frantically to stop, but it was too late.

Chapter Eight

OUT OF DANGER AND BACK AGAIN

" **O**h, no!" Josh cried in alarm as he slid straight toward Barrel. As the man reached for him, Josh dropped like a stone through the thick, grasping arms.

Barrel and Ox almost collided with each other as Josh rolled aside and sprang to his feet. He had only an instant to decide which way to run. The bougainvillea-covered fence on the left was too high to jump. The iron one on the right was ornamental and only about four feet high.

Josh asked himself, *Where's the surveillance team? Why aren't they helping me?*

As Ox and Barrel whirled around to grab again for Josh, he shot across the street toward the iron fence. There were spikes on the posts, but the top rail between posts had only small, decorative bumps. Josh leaped up, grabbed the rail, and threw himself over.

He landed on the lawn of a house, stumbled, caught himself, then sprinted alongside the house toward the sea.

Far behind, he could hear Tank yelling but couldn't tell

80

what he was saying. Closer behind, Josh heard the two men struggling to get over the iron fence.

Maybe, Josh told himself, *the surveillance people can't help me because they don't want anyone to know they exist! They're not after Ox and Barrel, but the man in the hat! Or maybe Sergeant Park didn't get his people set up in time, and they're not even watching! Guess I'll have to get out of this mess by myself!*

He dashed across the lawn and past the beautiful home with its manicured gardens. Ahead, his desperate eyes spotted a row of twenty-foot-tall, red and white oleanders marking the backyard boundary.

From behind, Josh heard Ox's voice call, "Stop, kid!" The chauffeur was obviously over the fence and running across the lawn after him.

Josh raced toward the oleanders, wondering if he could squeeze through them. If he could, what lay beyond? The sound of surf sounded ominously close.

There's a hole! Josh thought hopefully. He sprinted toward it, dropped to his knees, and plunged into the oleanders just as Ox's big fingers clutched at his basketball shoes. Josh jerked free and wiggled forward.

The hedge was about ten feet thick. Josh scrambled on hands and knees through a tunnel that had apparently been made by neighborhood kids. It was too small for Ox, who was yelling obscenities at the opening as he tried to squeeze his huge body through.

Josh cleared the oleanders and stood up, then let out

a startled "Oh!"

He was teetering on the edge of a small cliff. Six feet below that, wild surf boiled toward him, channeled between two small fingers of ancient volcanic rock. The blue green water leaped at him, gurgling strangely against the face of the cliff. Spray covered him as the wave dissolved into foam and retreated seaward.

Trapped! The thought screamed through his mind. *Those guys'll be through the oleanders in a minute!*

Josh glanced back. The hedge was too thick for him to see Ox and Barrel, but that meant they couldn't see him, either. He tried to catch his breath while frantically figuring out what to do next.

To the left, the open sea stretched toward the horizon. *Not that way!* he realized.

To the right, a great wall of lava had been forever frozen in time, making a mound too rough and steep to climb. *Not that way, either!*

Josh again looked down at the surf directly below, remembering the strange sound the water had made as it struck the cliff at his feet. He bent over, listening to a low, hollow, booming sound. Suddenly hopeful, Josh ran a few steps to the right and tried to peer under the cliff.

It looks a little like Five Graves on Maui, Josh thought. *If it is, maybe there's also a cave here! From the way the water's hitting that lava lip...*

He left his thought unfinished, remembering the site at Nahuna Point* on the neighboring island. Five Graves took its name from a few untended burial sites in the kiawe* that separated the road from the sea.

Five Graves was among several island sites where underwater caves had been made when lava tubes were formed during a primitive eruption. The red-hot magma inside had continued to flow while the outside was cooled faster by the seawater.

Eventually, the molten rock had emptied, leaving tubes and underwater caves. Scuba divers had proved that some tubes went back great distances under the land. But unless someone knew they were there, the caves would have been unnoticed.

At Five Graves, Josh also remembered foaming surf surging shoreward, making the same strange gurgling sound he heard moments before. The boy's mind jumped back to the spot where he now stood. *This sure looks like an underwater cave! Tide's out, so the water shouldn't come up too high inside.*

Josh glanced back and heard his pursuers angrily clawing their way through the oleanders. He looked down at the boiling surf below. *It'll be rough, but it's my only chance!*

Having decided that, he dropped to his backside and began sliding down on the lava, heading for the opening where the water surged and gurgled. When he got closer, he almost exclaimed aloud.

I was right! It is a small cave! I just need to get back in a couple of feet so they can't see me. I'll be okay if

I can keep from getting washed out by the retreating tide or being drowned when the water rushes in.

The boy held on to the rough volcanic rock with both hands and pulled himself into the tube's opening. He clung to the near wall so he would be less likely to be seen if either Ox or Barrel looked into the opening.

Josh gulped a quick breath and held it as the tide surged powerfully into his shelter. The sea exploded around him, covering him with tons of water and foam. Josh almost lost his finger hold as the water retreated. His head popped out, and he took a couple of deep breaths.

That's when he saw Ox. The chauffeur stood to the right on the lava mound above. He scratched his head with his right hand, then started turning toward Josh. The boy took another breath and crouched down, and the incoming tide covered him again.

Josh held on until the retreating water's force ripped his right hand loose from its grip on the lava. For a second, Josh thought he was going to be washed out of his hiding place right into full view of his pursuers.

The sea retreated rapidly, however, allowing Josh to regain his grip. He shook the water from his face and glanced up. Ox was gone.

Thank God! Josh breathed. *Now if both he and Barrel give up and go away before the tide gets too strong for me...*

Josh let the sea bury him twice more before he decided it was safe to take a look. As soon as the second wave drained away, the boy pulled himself forward so that he could see better.

There they are! Starting to crawl back through the oleanders! They've given up!

Josh scrambled up the wet, slippery volcanic mass to where he could see all around. He flopped face down on the top of the little cliff in the warm sun, catching his breath and waiting until he was sure the black limousine had driven off.

The salt water began drying on Josh's skin while he thought, *I sure hope Tank's okay!*

He was. Josh saw that a few minutes later when he eased through the oleanders again and ran past the house toward the iron fence.

Tank was trotting along in front of the bougainvilleas across the street, calling, "Josh? Where are you? They're gone! Josh! Answer me!"

"You're yelling so loud those guys will hear you and come back!" Josh said with a grin as he vaulted the fence.

"Where were you?" Tank demanded, running across the street toward Josh. "I saw them chase you in back of the house, and I could hear the waves crashing there! I thought you'd drowned! And from the look of your clothes, you almost did!"

"Well, I didn't, so stop worrying. Come on. Let's head back while I tell you what Kekoa told me about Duke."

Josh had finished recounting his conversation with Kekoa as the boys approached Waikiki.* The trade winds had completely dried Josh, leaving a sticky, salty feeling on his skin.

Tank prompted, "You said that Kekoa started to say Duke's mother was the only daughter of somebody when he was interrupted. He never finished telling you?"

"No."

"Maybe your theory's right about there being some kind of a tie between Duke and Chong."

"If there is, why did Duke get so upset when I mentioned it to him?"

Before Tank could answer, an old car pulled up beside them. Two surfboards were secured on top.

Duke leaned across the driver and called, "Hey, Josh! I was just going to meet you when I ran into a guy I used to know on the mainland. Come meet him."

Josh walked uneasily to the car. It was obvious that Kekoa hadn't delivered Josh's message. And why had Ox and Barrel been near Hidden Cove instead of being off somewhere so Josh and Duke could meet safely? Duke had said yesterday he'd see to that. Josh shook his head, trying to understand.

Bending to look inside at the driver, Josh saw he was a teenager—probably about a junior in high school. He had light red hair with countless freckles on his face, neck and arms.

"Hi," he said. "I'm Stu Hendricks."

"Josh Ladd. He's Tank Catlett."

"I was just starting for the north shore when I saw my

old mainland buddy walking along the street," Stu said. "He said he was going to meet you, so I offered him a ride. But since you're together now, why don't you jump in?"

Josh exchanged glances with Tank. Josh thought his best friend was thinking the same thing: *When had Duke been on the mainland, and how come Stu and Duke are going somewhere together without any apparent concern for Duke's usual "shadows"?*

Josh welcomed a chance to learn more about Duke, but he hesitated, remembering that the narcotics agent wanted Josh to stay away from Duke for a while. And Josh's father had said not to do anything that might cause the man in the limo to carry out his threat.

"Uh, thanks," Josh said, "but we can't."

Duke was unusually friendly. "Aw, come on, Josh! It'll give us a chance to talk!"

Tank didn't know about the narcotics officer's involvement or Mr. Ladd's instruction to stay away from Duke. So Tank urged, "Come on, Josh! Let's go home and get our boards!"

Tank raised his head from the car window so he wouldn't be overheard and whispered in Josh's ear, "Now's your chance to find out more of what Kekoa said."

Josh stalled, glancing around to see if there were any sign of Sergeant Park or his surveillance team. But Josh didn't really know what to look for, so his eager looking was useless.

An idea popped into his head. *I'll ask Mom, and she'll say no.* Aloud he said, "Well, we don't have our surf-boards, and we'd have to go ask our parents—"

"Jump in!" Duke interrupted. "Just tell ol' Stu how to find where you guys live."

"Yeah!" Stu added. "Let's go!"

Josh and Tank got in the back seat and directed Stu to drive toward Diamond Head. Duke turned in the front seat to look steadily and silently at Josh.

"Something wrong?" Josh asked, feeling uncom-fortable.

"Huh? Oh, no! No! I was just thinking how it must feel to have parents or someone else who really cares where you go and who else is along." Josh managed a smile. "Ox and Barrel care—at least, they sure keep an eye on you!"

Duke made a snorting noise of disgust and waved behind them. "Well, they won't bother me today!"

Tank laughed. "I can tell you why—uh!" His sentence broke off sharply as Josh jabbed an elbow into his friend's ribs.

Duke didn't seem to notice. He continued, "Yesterday I let them know I was going exploring in the Koolaus* this morning." He pointed to the volcanic mountains run-ning behind Honolulu. "Instead, I slipped out of my place to come meet you, Josh. Then I ran into Stu."

"Yeah!" the freckled teenager added. "I've been want-

ing to surf the north shore: Waimea Bay,* Sunset Beach
and the Banzai Pipeline!* I've heard that Waimea Bay has
the wildest waves in the world, especially in the winter!
Duke rides ten- to twelve-foot waves, but I'm not that
crazy, although I like to watch him do those wild things!"

Josh glanced out the rear window, wondering if a
surveillance team were following. He couldn't tell, but
at least the stretch limo wasn't behind them. Josh turned
around again.

"Where'd you know each other on the mainland?" he
asked.

Josh saw Duke's mouth set in a tight line, but Stu
laughed. "We were in the same foster home. Miserable
place! So we ran away together."

Josh wanted to ask, "Where do you live now, Duke?"
but Tank suddenly leaned forward.

"Duke," he said, "doesn't the person who pays for those
two men to watch you care about you?"

"He only cares about himself," Duke said bitterly.

"He?" Josh prompted.

Duke's face became a mask. "Nobody cares! Since my
parents died, I've had nobody who really cared about me.
Not one person!"

"I care," Josh said softly. "So does Tank. Maybe
Kekoa?"

Duke nodded slowly. "I know you two do," he said in
a near whisper. "But that old kanaka* is so wrapped up
in his search for his drowned grandson that he barely

notices me."

Josh wanted to say, "And you don't notice him, either," but instead he said aloud, "Well, at least Tank and I care."

"Don't forget me!" Stu chimed in. "At least, when we see each other, huh, Duke?"

In that moment, Josh was more determined than ever to be Duke's friend and to help him with whatever problem the men in the stretch limo presented.

Josh's mother was standing in the parking lot behind the apartments, talking to Tank's mother, when Stu drove up. Josh quickly introduced Duke and Stu and explained their request.

"Well," Mrs. Ladd said thoughtfully, glancing down the street where Josh had seen a light green sedan parked. "I suppose it's all right."

Josh's mouth nearly fell open in surprise as his mother turned to Tank's mother. Josh wanted to whisper, "But Mom, Dad said..." Instead he checked himself, thinking, *I guess Sergeant Park told her and Dad it's okay for me to be near Duke. Yeah! That makes sense! I'm sort of like bait! The narcotics people can't do anything unless Chong—or whoever he is—makes a move!*

Tank's mother gave her permission, too. Josh and Tank got their boards and secured them on top of the car with the other two. As the four boys turned onto the main street, Josh glanced behind. The same light green sedan pulled away from a be-still tree and followed Stu's car at a safe distance.

Josh sighed with relief. *That must be the surveillance people,* he thought. *Everything's going to be all right.*

Stu's car was through Honolulu and into open country when Josh glanced back again. He blinked in surprise. The green car was gone!

Chapter Nine

SOME STRANGE REVELATIONS

Tank, Stu and Duke were talking about surfing, but Josh had suddenly lost interest. He twisted in the back seat of Stu's car for a better look behind.

There's no car following! Josh told himself in disbelief. *Either the one I saw wasn't the surveillance team, or—hey! I know! Maybe a second car's following us now. I've seen that done on television. One car follows a while, then trades off with another so the people being followed don't get suspicious. Yeah! I see one back there that could be it!*

Semisatisfied that he'd solved the puzzle and the surveillance team was still behind him, Josh turned his attention back to the conversation.

Stu's car had passed the strange, reddish-colored earth that produced some of the world's finest pineapples. Now the road led northwest through gently rolling hills of sugarcane fields. They were on fire, with black smoke boiling into the sky. It was a common sight, for the leaves were always burned before harvest, leaving only the stalks.

Josh leaned forward to rest his arms on the back of the front seat between Stu and Duke. "It always amazes me that cane fields have to be burned every year," he said. "Why, some of those stalks are fifteen or twenty feet high! The way the trade winds blow so hard here, I'd be afraid the fires would get away and destroy the whole island."

Duke waved a tanned hand at the dark smoke and replied, "If it did get away, it'd just burn down to the water's edge and die out. It's perfectly safe. No houses or anything."

"I wouldn't want to be in a cane field when it's burning!" Stu said as he steered around a curve.

Tank interrupted. "Is that the ocean I see?"

"Yep!" Duke answered. "We're almost there!"

The gentle hills were left behind. The road led along flat stretches of land backing up from the ocean. Josh was struck again by the great beauty of the coves and beaches on Oahu's* north shore. The distant surf was modest. It wasn't at all like the wild waves of autumn and winter that bring champion surfers from around the world.

Stu parked beside a wild banana tree with its long, wide leaves. Josh stole a glance behind and down the quiet, paved road. He saw a car pull into the shade of another tree. Josh sighed, feeling sure that was the second car he had seen following.

Wish I could tell Tank! he thought as he carried his board across a stretch of brown and white sand beside the highway. The mighty Pacific Ocean's waves could rush straight into land there with nothing to slow them.

Today the sea was quiet. It was an almost totally flat expanse of deep blue spreading toward the horizon. "Doesn't look like much to me," Josh said with disappointment.

"Wrong time of the year!" Duke assured him. "But wait'll the storms start out in the Pacific later into the year. You'll see waves rushing in here so high they'll scare you just to look at them."

Josh's mind momentarily leaped away to what Kekoa had been telling him that morning before Tank's warning whistle had ended their conversation.

Who was Duke's mother? Josh wondered. *Kekoa said, "The only daughter of. . ." whom? Well, I'll get a chance to talk to Duke alone while we're waiting for a wave. I'd especially like to know how Richard Chong ties in to all this mystery.*

Tank and Stu eased over to the right to wait for a wave. Josh and Duke stayed behind.

"Thanks for inviting us," Josh began. He glanced around and added, "It's a peaceful spot."

"Yes, but danger's everywhere," Duke replied, pointing toward the shore.

Josh followed with his eyes. "You mean those tall posts with the tidal wave alert sirens?" They were everywhere on the island, even in the country.

Duke nodded. "At least we get warnings when tsunamis* are coming."

"You ever see a tidal wave, Duke?"

Duke let a small wave lift his board and pass on toward shore before answering. "No, but I've seen pictures of the damage they do. The newspaper some time back had shots of Hilo* after a tsunami. Parking meters twisted like paper clips. Buildings turned to splinters. But I'm not afraid. In fact, someday I'm going to catch one and ride it in."

"You're kidding!"

Duke shook his head. "I credit myself with riding an eighteen-foot wave already. The highest wave I've heard anybody surfing was a forty-five-footer. Guy was dropped from a helicopter out far enough to catch one that big."

"You're really not scared?"

Duke hesitated, then nodded. "I've been scared just seeing a big wave come toward me and realizing I was going to try riding it. But I made myself go ahead and do it. I get less scared each time. But so what? I've got nothing to lose if I ride a tsunami and fail."

"You could lose your life."

"That's what I said: I've got nothing much to lose."

"Your life's not important?"

Duke's reply was tinged with bitterness. "No, it isn't! What've I got to live for except surfing?"

"No family?" Josh knew the answer to that—at least he remembered what Kekoa had said. Duke had only one living relative. But who was that? Josh hoped to find out in the next few seconds.

"My parents moved from Hawaii to the mainland when I was little. They died there."

"I'm sorry."

Duke sighed. "For a few years I was bounced around from one foster home to another. I know there are some good ones, but not the ones where I was sent! To them, I was just a source of income. They got paid for having me there, but for nothing else. I was mistreated and unloved. So I kept running away. One time, with Stu."

Josh was surprised at the sudden, almost explosive flow of words from the other boy. Questions popped into Josh's mind, but he kept still, hoping Duke would say more.

Duke pulled his feet onto his surfboard. He didn't use a surf cord, Josh noticed again. He knew that was true of many top-level surfers.

Duke continued, "Then one day a private investigator showed up at my foster home. He had a wonderful story that sounded too good to be true."

The boy turned his head to look at Josh with eyes filled with pain. "It turned out I did have one living relative, my grandfather on my mother's side. After some paperwork and delays, I was brought back to Honolulu to live with him.

"I thought it was going to be great! But it wasn't. My grandfather was still bitter at my mother for having married a mainland haole* and running off to New York to live. He hated my father's memory even more. Naturally, I resented that. So my grandfather and I have had some nasty arguments the last few years."

Duke licked his lips, then said, "About that time I also learned some terrible truths about my grandfather. So I ran away again. But he won't leave me alone!"

Josh's memory flashed back to what the old Hawaiian had said, and Josh blurted out, "Your grandfather is Richard Chong, the pakalolo* godfather in these islands, isn't he?"

Too late, Josh remembered that once when he suggested a tie-in with Richard Chong, Duke had become angry and warned Josh to never say anything like that again.

But Duke seemed to have forgotten, too, or perhaps he was too startled at Josh's guess. "How'd you know?" he asked.

Josh shrugged. "Now it all makes sense! Your grandfather sees people as a threat to him when they become friendly with you, including Tank and me. He doesn't want you to have any friends so you'll come back to him. That's why those two muscle men follow you around. Am I right?"

Duke laughed, but without humor. "They're spies for my grandfather! They keep me prisoner—what my grandfather called 'a kind of house arrest'—and they also run off anybody who tries to be friends with me."

Josh let a wave lift both boards and pass shoreward before asking his next question. "If your grandfather's so mean, why does he let you do what you please, yet he won't let anyone be your friend?"

Duke didn't answer, so Josh continued. "Instead of having those two men keep you prisoner, as you put it, why doesn't he just kidnap you and lock you up? Since you're an orphan, nobody'd know what happened to you."

Duke idly ran a forefinger over the many stickers on his surfboard. "It's his way of forcing me to give up my life-style and move back with him. A week or two ago, he said that if I'd come back and live with him, he'd give me everything I want. But he won't, because I just want my freedom away from him.

"Besides, if I went back, he'd say nasty things about my parents again, and you can bet he'd want me involved in his business. He can't understand how I hate pakalolo!"

Josh nodded, finally understanding everything that had been going on since he first saw Duke. Then Josh's mind jumped to how Manuel had said Duke once seemed to lie about losing a surfing competition on purpose.

Josh studied the other boy, wondering, *Is Duke lying now?*

Suddenly, Duke pointed toward Tank and Stu. They were some distance away, waiting for a wave, their backs to Josh and Duke. Then Josh saw something else.

Shark!

The dark dorsal fin was between Josh, Duke and the other two boys. It extended about a foot and a half above the water.

Josh cupped his mouth to shout a warning, but Duke grabbed his hands. "Don't yell!" he said. "You may startle those guys and make them do something that'd cause the shark to think they're hurt or wounded. Then it would attack for sure!"

"But we can't just let that thing sneak up on them!" Josh protested.

He breathed a silent prayer and began paddling rapidly toward the shark, but with no idea of what could be done to protect his unsuspecting friend and Stu. *I wonder if it's a hammerhead, great white, tiger or white tip?* Josh mused. But then he realized, *It doesn't much matter— they're all dangerous!*

Josh was aware that Duke was paddling beside him as the great beast continued gliding silently behind Tank and Stu. Still ignorant of the shark's presence, they straddled their boards, legs dangling below on both sides.

Josh prayed silently, *Lord, what should I do?*

He didn't have to do anything. Slowly, Tank turned around and stiffened. Josh saw his friend's lips move, and Stu also whipped around, then froze.

"They've seen the shark!" Josh said hoarsely to Duke. "Now what?"

Josh and Duke were too far away to be of help, and Josh didn't know what could be done even if they were closer.

The great predator still swam straight for the other two boys, now stiff as the boards on which they sat.

Josh wanted to yell, "Don't move!" His own natural inclination would have been to jerk his feet out of the water. But surfboards don't offer safety. Sharks have been known to take two-foot sections out of them as easily as a boy bites an apple.

In horrified fascination, Josh watched the shark's high dorsal fin as it moved almost to the end of Tank's board, which was slightly closer and behind Stu's. The fin veered slightly to the left and came alongside Tank's dangling leg. Josh gulped and swallowed hard.

Abruptly, the shark turned away from the board and swam out to sea.

Josh let out a huge sigh of relief, and Duke exclaimed, "I've had enough surfing for today!"

On the drive back to Honolulu, Josh glanced periodically behind Stu's car, but there was no car that seemed to be following. Josh began to get a very uneasy feeling. *Something's wrong,* he told himself, *but what? Boy, I wish I could tell Tank what Sergeant Park said!*

As Stu's old car headed up the dead-end street toward the apartments where Josh and Tank lived, Josh turned to Duke in the front seat. "Where do you live?" he asked.

Duke seemed not to hear. "This was great, you guys!" he said. "Let's try to do it again soon."

Josh was disappointed, but he understood Duke didn't want to talk about his living arrangement. Josh got out of the car and glanced down the street. There was no other car that could have been following.

Something's really wrong! Josh told himself as he took his surfboard, called his thanks, and walked with Tank to their building. Josh found out what was wrong when his father came home from work.

"Sergeant Park called today and scared me half to death," Mr. Ladd explained. "He said there'd been a delay, and his surveillance team hadn't been able to start working on this case yet."

"What?" Josh said, gulping hard. "You mean they didn't follow. . .?"

His father continued, "When I called your mother and she told me you and Tank had gone to the north shore. . . Well, I'm sure glad to see you safely home!"

Josh's head was still reeling from the unexpected information. "Dad," he said, "I thought sure somebody was following us. But it must have just been coincidence."

Mr. Ladd changed the subject. "Son, tell me about your conversation with Duke today."

Josh recounted everything, including Duke's admission that Richard Chong was his grandfather.

When Josh had finished, his father frowned thoughtfully. "I don't like the way things are going. Son, tomorrow I'll drive you over near Waikiki.* Let's try to find that old Hawaiian. Maybe he can enlighten me on this situation, and perhaps I can help him deal with the loss of his grandson."

The next morning, Josh and his father found Kekoa walking toward Hidden Cove. Josh got out of the station wagon and greeted the old Hawaiian, then introduced him to his father. He invited Kekoa to get in so they could drive someplace to talk privately. Kekoa agreed, and the vehicle's springs sagged under the man's great bulk as he eased into the back seat.

As they drove toward Koko Head,* making small talk, Josh turned in his seat to face their passenger. "Yesterday Duke told me he's the grandson of Richard Chong, the pakalolo godfather in these islands," Josh said. "Is that true?"

Kekoa settled sad, brown eyes on the boy and nodded slowly. "Yes, his mother was Chong's only daughter."

Josh glanced at his father, thinking, *So everything else Duke told me yesterday was true, too! Now what?*

His father cleared his throat. "Thanks for confirming that, Kekoa," he said. "Now I'd like to ask you another very important question. How much danger do you think my son and his friend are in?"

"If you mean will Chong hurt them, I can only guess. He's a very powerful and determined man who's used to getting what he wants."

"I take that to mean there's a possibility that any friendship with Duke can be dangerous," Mr. Ladd said softly.

Josh started to protest, "Aw, Dad—"

"Kekoa," his father interrupted, "I'm sure you know my son would like to continue a relationship with Duke. But if it's risky. . ."

"How about if I see you, Kekoa?" Josh asked. "Would you be my friend?"

"Of course! But I'm afraid Chong would misunder-

stand. He'd think you were really trying to see Duke."
Josh realized that Kekoa was saying Josh would be unwise to go to the cove again to visit him or Duke. Josh's father seemed to grasp that, too. He changed the subject.

"Kekoa, yesterday I researched some old newspaper microfilm about tidal waves that have struck these islands in the past several years. I came across a story written thirteen years ago about a little boy named Akamu."

Mr. Ladd paused, glancing at his passenger in the rearview mirror. Kekoa took a deep breath and slowly let it out. "That was my grandson," he said. "Now, I am suddenly very weary. Please be so kind as to return me to Hidden Cove."

When they dropped Kekoa off where he wanted, disappointment settled over Josh and his father. Mr. Ladd sighed and said, "Guess we failed, Son."

Josh took a deep breath before answering, "Dad, I've got an idea."

"What's that?"

"I want to talk to Duke's grandfather!"

Chapter Ten

TROUBLE UPON TROUBLE

Josh's father almost choked in surprise. "What? Talk to Duke's grandfather? You mean, Richard Chong, the pakalolo* godfather?"

"Yes! If I could, maybe he'd leave Duke alone so he could live his own life, away from the crime and everything his grandfather represents."

"But Son, he threatened your life! And Tank's and our families'!"

"I know! But if it hadn't been for Duke..." Josh left the sentence unfinished because he'd said it often enough before.

"Son, I can understand the debt you feel you owe Duke, but talking to his grandfather?"

"When I almost drowned, I wanted to live. I still do. But from what I've learned, Duke's so unhappy he doesn't care whether he lives or dies. Maybe all the wild surfing he does is a way of escaping life—sort of accidentally. So he really needs help. He needs a friend! But his grandfather is keeping that from happening. Maybe I can talk him into letting me be Duke's friend."

"But Son, even if I'd agree to such an incredible idea, what would you say to this man?"

"I'd rather not tell you right now, but I've thought about it, and I think I know just what to say to make him let Duke go."

Josh reached out impulsively and gripped his father's hand where it rested on the steering wheel. "Don't you see, Dad? Meeting with Duke's grandfather is the only chance Duke has of being given his freedom! If Richard Chong does meet with me, I'll be safe, because Sergeant Park's men will be watching. They'll protect me."

"Something could go wrong!"

"Yes, but it could go right, too. Since it's the only way I know to help Duke, please let me try!"

Josh's father drove the rest of the way to the apartment in thoughtful silence. As he eased the station wagon under the carport, he finally replied.

"Son, assuming I'd even consent to such an idea, how would you meet this Richard Chong?"

"I'd ask Kekoa to send word through the men who watch Duke."

"I see. Well, I'd have to ask the narcotics agent's opinion, discuss it with your mother, and pray about it. So I'll let you know Sunday after church."

The church where the Ladd family worshiped was on a flat stretch of ground between the sea and the mountains. As Josh got out of the car to go to Sunday school that weekend, his eyes flickered past the flowering hibiscus and plumeria to touch the mountains behind.

They seemed to almost leap up from the flat land. Josh figured that when the last volcanic eruption had taken place countless centuries before, the lava had run to the left, toward downtown Honolulu. Lava folded over on itself and stayed that way instead of leveling out like settling mud. The magma had hardened so that an almost-vertical, two-hundred-foot cliff remained on the seaward side.

Tank came up behind Josh. "What're you looking at?" he asked.

"I was thinking about how that mountain formed."

Tank shaded his eyes against the morning sun. "All I see is some kiawe* growing on a lava mountain."

"I was thinking how powerful the volcano must have been to spit out all those miles and miles of melted rock. Yet it left flat places like this at the foot of the mountain that were made from much earlier flows."

Josh paused, then continued, "That's just a little example of what went on many centuries ago—and still goes on today on the Big Island. So think what it must have been like when God first began creating this whole chain of volcanic areas that make up the Hawaiian Islands."

"Boy, you're in a funny mood this morning!"

Josh dropped his eyes to meet those of his best friend. "If God made all those things and a whole lot more that was much harder than that—like the world and the

universe—He must have had a plan to build these islands."
Tank shrugged, puzzled by his friend's unusual conversation.

Josh continued, "But if somebody could have looked at those mountains up there—I mean, back when they were just melted, red-hot rocks flowing like chocolate cake batter when my mom's pouring it out—would anyone have guessed it would ever be anything except an ugly, black lava flow?"

"I don't understand you," Tank admitted.

"I'm coming to a point, so just answer my question. Would anyone have guessed back then—if there'd been anybody around—that someday all that heat and steam and lava would look like this?" He waved toward the beautiful, peaceful Hawaiian setting with the church in the middle.

"No, I guess not. But—"

"This morning when I was reading my Bible and looking over the Sunday school lesson again, I got to thinking about this thing with Duke and Kekoa and Chong."

Tank shook his head. "I'm still not following you."

"Just a second and you'll see it! Anyway, as I prayed and asked the Lord's help in what to do about this problem, I got to wondering if it's really true that God is sovereign."

"Our Sunday school teacher says He is. He made a pretty good case for it from the Bible. But what's that got to do with Duke and the others?"

"Well, when I got out of the car today and saw these mountains, I thought about what I just told you. Back when it was happening, it didn't look as if anything good could ever come from all that hot lava. Dad once called it 'chaos.' But now the result is so perfect that people call this place 'paradise.' See?"

Tank looked up at the mountain and then back to his friend. "Are you saying that you think some good's going to come out of all this mess with Duke and Chong?"

"If I didn't, I guess I'd get discouraged and quit trying. As it is, I'm getting curious to know how it's going to turn out."

"Well, I'm more anxious to stay out of trouble right now. Play it safe so those threats aren't carried out."

Josh smiled at his friend. "That's why we're such a good combination. You're too cautious!"

"And you're too much the other way, Josh!"

"Maybe so, but I think my prayers are going to be answered. This whole thing with Duke's going to turn out fine. You'll see."

Josh turned and started walking toward the church. Tank swung in beside him. Josh wanted very much to tell Tank about the surveillance teams, since he didn't like keeping secrets from his best friend. But he had to honor the narcotics agent's request.

"A lot will depend on whether Dad decides to let me send a message to Chong," Josh said.

"What do you think he'll decide?"

"I don't know. All we can do is wait." He took another couple of steps, then added, "And pray."

That night, Josh's father looked at him over the top of his silver half-glasses and announced his decision. "Your mother and I have prayed about letting you meet with Richard Chong. I also talked to Sergeant Park about the idea. He said his surveillance teams are now ready, so they'll be watching you. If you still want to try meeting with Chong, I'll go with you to Hidden Cove while you deliver the message."

The next morning, Josh and his father found Kekoa just as he started across Waikiki* Beach to sit by the shore.

Josh told the old Hawaiian the message he wanted delivered to Duke's grandfather through the two muscular guardians.

"I'm sure you've all carefully considered the risks involved in sending such a message?" Kekoa asked.

Josh's father nodded. "We have. We've decided that Josh's plan is worth a try."

"Then I'll send the message."

"Thanks," Josh said, starting to turn away. Then he spun back to face Kekoa.

"If this doesn't work and Duke's grandfather refuses to let him be friends with Tank and me, I wouldn't like to see Duke be without someone who cares. Are you sure you won't change your mind and be his friend? Then you'd both have somebody. Right now, neither of you has anyone."

"No, my young friend. I must wait for the sea to give back what it took. I'm sorry."

Josh nodded his understanding. "Me, too. Well, see you later."

"Wait!" Kekoa's word made father and son stop to look expectantly at the old Hawaiian. "Mr. Ladd, I'm becoming rather fond of your adventuresome son. Would you mind if he stayed and talked with me for a while?"

Father and son exchanged glances, then looked around. Both knew that somewhere nearby the narcotics officers were watching. They could have been in a car or van parked at the curb, on one of the hotel lanais* overlooking the beach, or even somewhere on the sand itself, pretending to be tourists.

Josh's father replied, "This is a public beach, so I suppose it's all right. But don't go near Hidden Cove, Josh."

When his father had gone, Josh sat down on the sand beside Kekoa. The boy felt good about the invitation to stay. Josh also felt safe knowing the surveillance team was watching.

"Have you ever seen where Duke lives?" Josh asked.

"Yes. He has a room in a small house owned by a widow. He does odd jobs for her in exchange for food, lodging and some spending money."

"Doesn't she wonder that he has no guardian?"

"She knows he's a runaway orphan from the mainland, but she doesn't pry, and he doesn't tell more than that."

Kekoa stood up and brushed sand off the seat of his old

cutoffs. "Let's walk and talk, my inquisitive friend."

As they walked along the shoreline, Josh smiled and asked, "Where'd you learn to talk that way?"

"Watching the sea is lonely work, so I began bringing books to read. Then I started using some of the words I'd learned, and this impressed people. That pleased me, so I kept doing it. We all like compliments."

Josh agreed as his mind jumped to what would happen to Duke if there were no meeting with Richard Chong—or if Chong refused to let Duke go. "I wish you'd reconsider being Duke's friend," he said.

"I can't do that. Besides waiting for my grandson, there's another reason."

"Oh?"

Kekoa glanced seaward, then continued. "Suppose Duke and I did become friends. Because of our ages, I'd be like a grandfather and he like a grandson. But the wild way he rides the board can only end in disaster. Sooner or later, it will happen, and I cannot bear to have the sea take another life from me."

Josh felt a sudden urgency to help Duke before his recklessness claimed his life. But how?

Kekoa added quietly, "Then I would be alone again."

"But everybody runs that same risk," Josh protested, "loving somebody, yet knowing sooner or later they'll be parted. It's the times in between that make it all worthwhile. The loving, the friendship. . ."

"You are wise beyond your years, my blue-eyed, young

friend!"

"Thanks." Josh glanced inland and stiffened. "There's the limo!"

Kekoa stopped and followed the boy's eyes. "That means Duke must be nearby," he said. "Perhaps in Hidden Cove."

Josh felt nervous, knowing that behind the darkened windows of the stretch limo, he was being watched. Then Josh relaxed, remembering that somewhere close by, Sergeant Park's officers were also watching.

The two turned and walked back toward their starting point. They sat down on the sand again as Kekoa pointed and said, "There's Duke. See? Just passing the lava point leading away from Hidden Cove."

The fluorescent green trunks were unmistakable. Duke also wore a bright orange jersey. He paddled out toward the breaking waves, alone as usual.

Man and boy continued to watch as Duke reached the surf and straddled his board, waiting for a wave. "Are you a good surfer?" Kekoa asked Josh.

"No, not really. I'm still learning."

"You can learn from watching Duke." The old Hawaiian again looked seaward. "He's ready to ride. Watch him as he does the four basic maneuvers."

Josh looked to where Duke was waiting. He knew that waves come in sets of two to four, followed by a couple of minutes' lull. He could see a set coming; they were about three feet high. That wasn't big surf, but it was just right for the most fun riding a hard board.

Kekoa explained, "The first maneuver is called the takeoff. That's when he'll catch the wave and take the drop down to the bottom. It'll happen very quickly, so look sharp!"

Josh saw Duke push up evenly with both hands on the board. He instantly leaped to his feet as the wave swelled and neared its peak. In one fluid motion, Duke placed his "goofy foot" forward on the board. His knees were slightly bent, arms moving freely for balance.

Next Duke slid down the face of the wave before it broke and tumbled over itself. The drop to the bottom was very fast.

"Now the second maneuver!" Kekoa exclaimed. "The bottom turn! See?"

Josh watched Duke turn sharply away from the breaking wave, moving to the watchers' left.

"Here's the third maneuver!" Kekoa said. "The trim! That's when the surfer rides parallel to the breaking curl. He's also riding away from the white water. See?"

Josh could only nod before Kekoa spoke again. "Now the fourth maneuver: the cutback. See how he's reversing direction and cutting back toward the curl but staying in the wave?"

"Wow!" Josh exclaimed. "I learned a little about those moves when I first started surfing, but I've never seen them done so fast! It's almost as if Duke combined all four maneuvers into one!"

"He's so very good, but he's also reckless. That's why I fear for his life. So I do hope that when your message is sent to the pakalolo godfather, he'll meet with you to— what's the matter?"

Josh had tensed, looking down the beach. He felt his heartbeat increase. "Here comes Barrel and your chance to deliver my message," he said, "but I'd better go!"

Standing with forced casualness so the approaching muscle man wouldn't think he was afraid, Josh glanced toward the street. What he saw made his heart jump to an even faster tempo.

The limo was gone! Did that mean Ox, the chauffeur, was waiting to intercept him somewhere away from the beach? And was Richard Chong with Ox?

"See you later, Kekoa," Josh said as he walked at a right angle away from Barrel and toward the street. "Please see that my message is delivered."

"Rest assured that it will be done, my compassionate friend."

Josh tried not to hurry as he moved across the sand. Out of the corner of his eye, he could see that Barrel was still approaching the old Hawaiian and not following him. Flicking his eyes up and down the street, he thought, *Where's the limo?*

Josh felt his mouth go dry, wondering if Sergeant Park's surveillance people had followed the limo. Were there enough officers to also keep an eye on him?

He walked warily off the beach and onto the street, his

mind whirling. *Will Duke's grandfather meet with me? What if he will but doesn't like what I say?* The short hairs on the back of his neck began to tingle. *What've I done? Will it only make matters worse?*

The boy shivered even though it was a warm, muggy summer day.

Chapter Eleven

DANGER IN A CANE FIELD

Josh crossed Kalakaua* Avenue and started up the street toward home. He glanced back and saw Barrel talking to Kekoa. *My message to Duke's grandfather is on its way,* he thought. *Wonder when—or if—I'll hear from him?*

Josh kept a wary eye out for the black limo. Then he saw it moving slowly down the street toward him. His tendency was to run home, but he forced himself to walk casually.

He avoided glancing back again to see if he could locate the narcotics agents' vehicle following the limo. *Ox might catch on if he saw me acting suspiciously,* he reasoned.

There was nothing to do but try to ease his speeding heart and keep walking. The limo didn't pass. Only when he came to the dead-end street leading to his apartment could he risk a sideways glance to check on the car's location.

Not there! Josh heaved a sigh of relief. *Didn't follow me all the way! But it's not over! It can't be until I find out if Richard Chong will meet with me.*

Josh forced himself to stop short of adding the negative thought that wanted to express itself: *Even if Chong meets with me, he'll never listen to me!*

Over the next two days, it was hard for Josh not to reveal everything to Tank. The boys stayed away from Waikiki,* although Tank was suspicious.

"What's wrong?" Tank asked the second day. "You're nervous as a mongoose!*"

"I'm...waiting. I can't tell you any more. Later, I'll explain why."

"Does it have anything to do with the man who came to your apartment a few days ago?"

Josh blinked in surprise but didn't answer.

"Roger's grandmother saw him and asked me," Tank explained. "How come you didn't tell me about him?"

"I can't!"

"I thought we were friends without any secrets!"

Josh took a deep breath, thinking fast. "Aren't we good enough friends that you can trust me until I can tell you?"

"Guess so, but it'd better be soon!"

On the third night, Josh's father reported that he had met secretly with Sergeant Park. The narcotics teams had nothing to report, so the surveillances continued.

Mr. Ladd concluded, "They're waiting for a break. Maybe that'll come when you hear whether Richard Chong agrees to meet with you."

Josh awoke on the fourth day with a sense of desperation. *I've got to know if Duke's grandfather's going to meet with me! Maybe Kekoa's heard something!*

He dressed in an old, rust-colored tee shirt, summer slacks and basketball shoes without socks. He wanted Tank to accompany him to Waikiki Beach, but Tank had a dental appointment and couldn't go. So Josh went alone, wondering if a surveillance vehicle was following him.

As he approached the beach, he suddenly stopped dead still. A mournful wailing sound started to fill the air.

"Oh, no! Not again!" Josh exclaimed aloud.

For a moment, Josh wanted to deny that the tidal wave alert sirens were sounding, but that wasn't possible. Although he felt anxious, he told himself, *It's probably just another false alarm. Still, I'd better get home so Mom won't worry.* He turned and started retracing his steps.

Josh was sorry not to be able to ask Kekoa if he'd heard any response from Richard Chong. But Josh was more concerned about the tsunami* warning.

He was about halfway home when he heard a car slow behind him. Josh glanced back just as the black limo eased to a stop at the curb. His mouth suddenly went dry as he recognized Ox through the windshield.

The rear passenger door swung open, and a man's voice said softly yet with authority, "Get in, Josh!"

The boy wanted to run, but he held himself in check, trying to see into the darkened interior. He shook his head and said, "I'm not allowed to get into cars with strangers."

He caught a glimpse of an expensive straw hat that he

recognized instantly. "You sent a message, Josh!" the man said. "You wanted to talk! Now get in!" The voice wasn't controlled as it had been when the "final warning" was given. Now it was harsh and strong.

The boy shook his head. "I'll stand here and—"

Ox was out from behind the wheel so quickly that Josh had barely turned and started to run when he was grabbed. Powerful arms dropped over his shoulders.

Josh glanced desperately up and down the street, wondering if the surveillance officers were watching. A couple of blocks behind, he saw two men in the front seat of a white van who seemed aware of Josh's situation. *Hope one of them is Sergeant Park!* he thought.

Seconds later, kicking uselessly, Josh was shoved onto a rear-facing seat in the back of the limo. The door slammed, and the lock clicked.

Josh turned defiantly to the man facing him. "Kidnapping's a federal offense!" Josh cried, trying not to sound scared. "You could—"

"This isn't a kidnapping!" the man interrupted. His voice was cool, soft again. "You sent word to me! You ride along peacefully and say what's on your mind, and I'll bring you back here safe and sound."

The limo eased away from the curb and back into traffic. "Otherwise," the man added quietly, "I'm dumping you out right here and now! So do you want to talk or not?"

Josh was flustered. He looked past the man's head through the darkened rear window. The white van had pulled away from the curb and was following a block behind. Josh took a deep breath and tried to calm down. *The surveillance crew's close by!* he assured himself. *Nothing can happen.*

Aloud he said, "Yes, I want to talk, but not now! The tidal wave alert sirens are sounding!"

"Probably just another false alarm. Now make up your mind!"

Josh took a slow breath, thinking fast. "Okay," he said, letting out the breath. "But we stay close to here. All right?"

"We won't go far."

By now, Josh's eyes had adjusted to the soft interior light, so he could see the eyes under the hat brim.

"You're Richard Chong, Duke's grandfather?"

The man nodded briefly but snapped, "His name isn't Duke! That's some stupid name he chose for himself!"

Josh swallowed, feeling the man's hostility and knowing that wasn't the way to get what he wanted. "What do you want me to call him?" he asked.

"It doesn't matter, I guess. Call him Duke if you want."

The pakalolo* godfather was nothing like the caricature of Asian villains Josh had seen in films. Chong was about sixty and big for an Oriental, with a round, almost-cherubic face. His clothes were expensive and smelled faintly of cigars. He looked much like the many successful Chinese-American businessmen around Honolulu, except for the eyes. They were bright and hard.

Josh remained silent a moment, sensing the anger easing out of Chong. "What'd you want to see me about, Josh?" the man asked.

"I...I wanted to ask you to please let me be friends with Duke. My friend Tank, too."

There was a pause, then Chong asked softly, "That's it?"

"Well, I've got my reasons, but I wanted to say that part first in case you didn't listen."

Chong leaned forward so his brown eyes were within inches of the boy's blue ones. "Listen, Josh," he said. "This is none of your concern. You've got family and friends. Duke, as you call him, is all I've got! Now, is it too much to ask you to stay away from him?"

Josh tried not to flinch. He stared steadily back into the cold eyes and asked the question he had been pondering for days: "Do you love your grandson?"

Chong jerked backward as though Josh had jabbed him with a pin. "What?" he exclaimed.

"I asked if you love your grandson."

"Of course!"

Josh hesitated, licking his lips. "How much do you love him, Mr. Chong?"

"I don't have to answer that question!"

"Of course not, but I want you to think about it. Do you really love your grandson, or do you want him around as you might want a pet dog or something?"

The dark eyes glittered with a strange light as the man

leaned forward. "I resent that, you smart-mouthed kid!"

Josh was terribly frightened, but he plunged ahead to say, "I'm sorry, but it's a fair question. If you really love your grandson, you'd do anything for him, wouldn't you?"

The glitter softened in the eyes. "So?"

"So do you love him enough to give him his freedom?"

"What?"

"From what Duke told me, all you've brought into his life is trouble and pain! You bad-mouthed the memory of his mother—your own daughter! You said things about his father that hurt him. He ran away, but you won't leave him alone.

"You're trying to take the only thing he loves in life— being free to surf and make his own friends—and drag him back into your life, which is nothing but trouble and always will be!"

For a moment, Josh thought Chong was going to strike him. Instead he suggested, "Sit back and relax while I give this some thought, Josh."

Reluctantly, the boy obeyed. He glanced out the side windows and realized they were moving through downtown Honolulu toward the north shore. He started to protest that they weren't staying close to his apartment as Chong had promised. But then he thought better of it and kept quiet. Looking out the back window as casually as possible, he saw the white van was still trailing them.

They were into the country now, passing pineapple

fields with their strange-colored earth, when the pakalolo godfather took a deep breath and spoke again.

"You got anything else to say, Josh?"

Josh swallowed, concerned that the man hadn't answered his question about letting Duke go. Josh shot another look out the back window, then blinked.

The white van pulled over to the side of the road. Sudden concern seized Josh. *Maybe they've got car trouble!* he thought. *Or maybe they're switching cars. Another will follow us now so Ox doesn't get suspicious.*

The boy saw a nondescript, gray sedan pull out of a side road and swing into traffic behind the limo. Josh relaxed, feeling confident other surveillance officers were following in the second vehicle.

Josh took a deep breath and spoke again. "Yes, I've got something else to say, Mr. Chong. The way he's going, Duke'll probably get killed surfing. But if you'd leave him alone, he'd find a reason for wanting to live. He could make friends the way he wants. Maybe he'd even get friendly with the old Hawaiian Kekoa."

"That nutty old man? Why should anyone want to be friends with him?"

"He's not crazy, Mr. Chong. He's just a little 'off' on one subject. He and Duke could be friends. Oh, I know you could give Duke wealth and all that, but what he needs is somebody to love him—unselfishly—to care enough to let him go if that's best."

Josh concluded quietly, "Do you love him that much?"

Chong turned abruptly toward the driver. "Take the nearest side road," he said.

Startled, Josh looked out the window as Ox whipped the limo onto a dirt road. A rooster tail of dust leaped up, but not before Josh realized they were driving rapidly through acres of very tall sugarcane stalks.

"What—" Josh started to ask as the limo stopped.

Chong reached past Josh and shoved the door open. "Get out!" he ordered.

"But you said—"

"Out!"

Ox ran around from the driver's side and jerked the boy from the rear seat onto the dirt road. He fell backward, suddenly understanding how Duke would not have gotten along with his strong-willed, self-serving grandparent.

Josh heard the trade winds rattling the tall stalks. They bent at a sharp angle, showing the strength of the trades.

"You can't just leave me out here!" Josh cried. He scrambled to his feet. "There's a tidal wave alert! And I don't know where I am!"

Neither man answered. Ox closed the back door, but not before Josh saw Chong had turned away. The chauffeur hurried around the front of the limo and back inside.

"Wait!" Josh yelled. "Take me to—"

The driver's door slammed solidly shut. The vehicle roared away in a cloud of dust.

Josh suddenly remembered the gray sedan. It wasn't

in sight. Neither was any other vehicle. There was only settling dust left by the limo.

Josh prayed silently, *Lord, I hope they didn't lose me!* He turned to glance hopefully in every direction. *Got to find some help!* But instantly he knew there was nothing—no house, storage shed, car, person or telephone booth. He was in the middle of miles of unending cane fields with stalks growing fifteen to twenty feet high.

All Josh heard was the low moaning of the wind and the rattling of dry leaves. The cane bent and parted slightly. Through the break and at the far end of the dirt road, Josh glimpsed a low-lying section of the ocean.

It was peaceful, calm and beautiful. Silver flecks danced where the sun hit the waves. Far out, the surf broke in graceful shades of emerald green and foaming white.

Wonder if the tidal wave alert I heard was another false alarm? he asked himself. *The sirens sounded some time ago, so if there is a real tsunami, it could be getting close! This ground's so flat that a tidal wave would surely come up this far!*

He tried not to think more, but the words seemed to shriek in his mind: *I'd be swept out to sea like Kekoa's grandson!*

Josh stared at the ocean, half-expecting to see a giant wave rise up out of the tranquil sea, swell to the height of a six-story building, then rush toward him.

On shore, something moved, catching the boy's eye. He focused on a small, twisting wisp of something where he'd last seen the limo.

Recognition struck, and his heart almost stopped.

Smoke! The word exploded in the boy's mind. *Two, three—no, five spots! Somebody's set the cane field on fire! The wind's sweeping it right toward me!*

Chapter Twelve

A RUN FOR LIFE

Josh instinctively took a step back, watching the burning cane as it exploded on a wide front. It raced toward him ahead of the stiff trade winds.

"Got to get out of here!" he exclaimed aloud.

Still, he couldn't seem to take his eyes off the danger heading toward him. Heavy, black smoke trailed ugly tentacles across the sky, then erupted into a massive cloud. Yellow tongues of fire, wild and hungry, licked outward, causing everything they touched to burst into flames.

Josh saw evidence of the danger at once. A flash of brown over to one side made the boy glance down. A mongoose, apparently whiffing the smoke, dashed away, seeking safety that would not be found anywhere in the field.

Which way's best? Josh asked himself as he scanned the area. *There!* Inland, visible through another wind-blown break in the cane, a tall, green mound marked the beginning of the mountains and the end of the field. *That's the highest ground!*

He ran a few quick steps toward the mountain, intending to plunge through the towering cane. But the first rough, dry leaves stopped him.

Can't get through there! Well, I'm probably safer on this dirt road anyway. But I need to find a path that goes closer to that mound! He started running at right angles to his goal. Dust spurted from under his feet. The fire gained rapidly. Josh turned from time to time and soon saw by the smoke that the five original fires had grown together in a single front.

I wonder if Chong set it? he thought. *Or Ox? No! They wouldn't do anything that terrible, knowing I'm in here. Or would they?* He quickly decided it did no good at the moment to speculate on who set the fire.

As he ran, Josh's eyes probed for an intersecting road leading toward his objective. *Slow down!* he cautioned himself, puffing hard and feeling the pounding of his heart. *There's time! Save my strength for the long haul!*

He continued to jog, glancing back often. The fire now advanced on a half-mile-wide front, racing toward him with surprising speed. Curling, black smoke formed an ugly scum of a cloud overhead. Little pieces of ash drifted down around Josh like black snowflakes.

Breathing hard, Josh swiveled his head for another backward glance. A flash of sunlight on metal reflected momentarily.

That's the limo! Driving along the highway by the sea!
The swirling smoke hid the vehicle. Josh's eyes dropped

to the leaping flames again. *They're making pincers, going faster on the right and left of me!*

Fearful the fire might overtake him, Josh again broke into a full run. Ahead, he glimpsed another dirt road intersecting the one he was on.

Great! he thought with a flash of relief. *Goes right toward the mountain at the edge of the cane field! If I can just—*

He almost stumbled over a cane rat running in panic. At the same instant, Josh saw the largest spider he'd ever seen. It dragged itself from among the standing cane into the road. *I've heard cane spiders were large, but this one's bigger'n anything I ever saw!*

Now Josh tried to keep himself from looking back, because each time he did, he could see the fire was gaining. The smoke burned his lungs, and he fought an urge to cough.

Behind the burning field, the sea still stretched out peacefully in shimmering silver, glistening jade and foaming white. Then, as Josh watched, it changed.

He had seen countless waves form, building a few feet to peak and crest before rushing shoreward. But he had never seen anything like this!

It started like any wave—rising, building, building—but it didn't crest. It rose higher and higher until the low-lying clouds on the horizon were blocked from view.

Tidal wave!

Josh stopped running, frozen in utter fascination. Next

the wave moved shoreward, slowly at first, then faster and faster until it was a roaring mountain that seemed to shake the ground where Josh stood.

The tsunami* smashed ashore like a solid wall. The trees marking the roadway and the beach bent and disappeared. The wall rushed on, falling forward on itself. Everything before it vanished as though it had never existed. "Oh, no! Lord, please!" Josh cried aloud as he turned to run flat-out, wildly pouring everything he had left into a desperate dash to the hill.

The roar behind him was terrible. It was worse than all the pounding surfs and thundering seas he had ever heard. Then the noise changed. A strange hissing sound made Josh jerk his head around to see.

Acres of flaming sugarcane leaves directly behind Josh vanished into steam. Still, the roaring fire on both sides of Josh plunged on, threatening to encircle him. He could feel the scorching heat on his back. His frantic eyes saw that the tidal wave was surging toward him, its mighty power still unchecked.

Something hit Josh's feet, and he stumbled. He swiveled around, arms outstretched in a vain effort to break his fall. Out of the corner of his eye, he saw another mongoose flash into the cane and knew that's what had tripped him.

"Noo!" Josh cried as he fell forward into the dirt road, cutting his hands on sharp pebbles. He tried instantly to scramble up, but his right ankle wouldn't hold him.

Collapsing in pain, he grabbed for the ankle and spun half around. The fire on both sides was within thirty feet of him. And the tidal wave was still rushing toward him as well.

Almost on top of me!

Josh threw himself onto hands and knees and began crawling desperately through the red dust. But the hill was too far away.

I'll never make it! he realized.

Then the wave was upon him.

Josh felt the onrushing tidal wave seize his left shoe— the one farther behind him. The water soaked his pants leg.

Desperately, with labored breathing and fear for his life, he pulled his left foot even with his right. He grimaced at the pain in that ankle. Yet he hadn't felt the water soak his second shoe or that pants legs.

He didn't consciously think about that, however. Choking and coughing on the smoke and half-sobbing in desperation, Josh dug his fingers into the reddish-black dust and scrambled forward on all fours.

He expected to feel the water crash over him and throw him forward like a cork on the wave. When it slowed, he knew the water would suck him back at jet speed to the vast, open sea. He'd disappear as Kekoa's grandson had done.

Still scrambling forward, Josh felt a panicked cane rat dash across his outstretched hand. He barely noticed it in his own clawing efforts to keep going toward high ground.

A hissing of steam told him the last of the fire had been doused. He heard the surging water just behind him, and he cringed, bracing himself against the expected impact of the wave.

But it didn't happen. Instead, the terrible roaring of the tidal wave slowed. Josh jerked his head around to look behind him. The wave had reached its farthest point inland. The water again licked tentatively at Josh's left foot and soaked his pants leg.

Then, slowly, the water inched backward. It slithered, as if reluctantly, toward the sea. Next, as Josh watched in relieved disbelief, the retreating wave became a mighty, rushing torrent. It roared like a giant waterfall as it carried everything in it at incredible speed back toward the cradle where it had been born.

Josh watched it go, then glanced down in wonder. *I'm still alive!*

His left leg was wet to the knee. His right ankle was painful but dry. Josh's bleeding hands were in dry dirt, but the road at his feet glistened with newly created mud.

The tops of cane stalks on both sides of the boy poured steam, but the fire was out. Both dangers had passed.

Still breathing hard, Josh dropped wearily on his backside in the dust and mud. He stared in relief as the water surged in a great sucking sound toward the sea. The wave carried uprooted and blackened cane stalks with other debris.

It left behind a devastated cane field and one very scared, tired but grateful boy. He looked up and panted, "Thanks—again, Lord!"

Wearily, Josh glanced at his injured right ankle. *Maybe there's another wave!* he cautioned himself. *I'd better get to that mound, just in case the next wave's bigger.*

He half-crawled, half-hobbled onward and upward. He was scratched and sore, muddy and smelling of smoke and dust when he dragged himself to the top of the mound. He collapsed to catch his breath and ease his injured hands and ankle, then blinked in surprise. He stared down.

Off to the left of the devastated cane field, a cloud of dust marked the rapid approach of a vehicle on the dirt road the water had not touched.

It's that same van! The words leaped to Josh's mind. *The surveillance people! They must've had car trouble or something and were delayed!*

Josh tried to stand but couldn't. He pushed himself to one knee and waved. Between gasps for air he shouted, "I'm up here!"

A horn honked three times in recognition, and the headlights flashed.

Josh felt sudden, hot tears of relief forming behind his eyes. He slowly collapsed onto the grassy knoll and waited for the surveillance crew to reach him.

It was over—well, almost.

Later at home, with his ankle treated and bandaged,

Josh told everyone about the surveillance arrangements and how Sergeant Park's men had rescued him from the hilltop. Eventually, Josh began running out of details to tell his audience of relieved family and friends.

Finally he said, "Oh, I just remembered! There's one more thing. You know what I thought about when those plainclothes narcotics officers were helping me into their van? I wondered if Duke really tried to ride the tsunami on his surfboard. I know it's crazy, but that's what I thought!"

Josh's father pursed his lips thoughtfully. "Too bad those surveillance people had a flat tire when they were following you and Chong," he said. "This whole terrible experience might have been avoided."

"Yeah," Josh admitted, "but as I told Tank at church the other day, I felt it was all going to turn out okay." Then he added, "Dad, I've got to know what happened to Duke and Kekoa. Could you take me to see them, please? It's safe now."

A little later, Josh leaned on his father and Tank to limp through the kiawe* toward Hidden Cove. With rising anxiety, Josh stood at last on the edge of the thorny trees.

There he stopped dead still and sucked in his breath. "Wow! Dad! Tank!" he exclaimed. "Look at this place!"

Below them, the twin palm trees were gone. The beach at the end of the kiawe was gone, leaving only ancient, black, volcanic bedrock. The entire beautiful, white, sandy area was a debris-covered scene of total destruction.

Tank whispered in awe, "It's all been wiped out!"

Josh's heart seemed to lurch into his throat as he glanced away. "Duke! Kekoa!" he cried. "If they were here when it hit . . ."

Josh couldn't finish the thought. He glanced wildly around and suddenly felt sick inside.

There was no sign of life anywhere.

Chapter Thirteen

THE SECRET OF HIDDEN COVE

Josh resisted the feeling that he was going to be sick at what he saw. He stumbled slightly on his injured right ankle as he spun again to search the desolation.

"Dad! Tank!" he shouted. "The whole thing's gone! The tidal wave took everything right down to the original lava flow!"

"Not quite, my anxious young friend!"

Josh swiveled his head toward the voice. "Kekoa!"

"Aloha!*" the old Hawaiian replied. He waved from Josh's left and pushed himself up from where he had been sitting on a volcanic outcropping high above the sea.

"Hi!" Josh yelled with great relief. "Where's Duke?"

"Right here!" The tall boy straightened up from just beyond Kekoa.

"You both okay?" Josh asked.

"Fine!" Duke replied. "What happened to your foot?"

"Tell you later!"

Josh hobbled as quickly as his injured ankle would permit along the bare, black lava that had been uncovered by the tidal wave. Duke and Kekoa hurried toward him. When they met, Josh reached out impulsively and gave Duke a hug. "Boy, you don't know how glad I am to see you!" he said.

"Same here," Duke said, his voice a little husky.

Josh released Duke and opened his arms to Kekoa. It was like reaching around a grain silo because the man was so big. Kekoa almost crushed Josh in returning the hug.

Then everyone joined in a spontaneous round of joyful bear hugs and slapping each other on the back.

When the first emotional outburst was over, Josh faced Duke and Kekoa. "Where were you two when the tsunami* hit?" he asked.

Duke smiled and said, "I rode the wave in!"

"You didn't!" Josh exclaimed.

Duke's smile widened to a grin. "Well, not really the big one." He waved at the devastation. "Not the one that did this. But I managed to catch at least a twenty-footer that seemed to be the forerunner of the big one."

"I didn't know there was more than one!" Tank said.

"Two hit here!" Duke assured him. "I was sitting on this high ground with Kekoa when the really big—and final—one did this." He waved toward the wasteland that had been a crescent-shaped, white-sand beach.

Kekoa added, "Wait'll you hear the whole story!"

"Tell us!" Josh urged.

"Kekoa was sitting there as always, watching," Duke

explained, "when I came shooting in on that wave. He told me when I got ashore—uh, why don't you tell them, Kekoa?"

Josh stared in bewilderment at the two grinning people before him.

The old Hawaiian's face sobered. He looked straight at Josh and lowered his voice. "The kahuna* was right, my audacious young friend! The sea returned my grandson to me!"

"What?" Josh exclaimed as he pulled back in surprise. Had Kekoa totally lost his mind?

Kekoa reached out and placed a big hand on Duke's arm. "I had been thinking of what you said, Josh, but it took me a long time to accept it. Then, when I saw Duke riding in on that first tidal wave, I realized a great truth."

"What's that?" Josh asked, not understanding.

Kekoa's voice dropped and became husky. "You suggested something that Duke and I might do, but I wouldn't listen. You see, I had been looking for something when it was already before me." He pulled Duke close. "I mean, this is the grandson for whom I've been waiting."

"And Kekoa is my tutu kane makua,*" Duke replied quietly. "At least," he added with a smile, "he's my calabash* grandfather."

Josh swallowed hard, feeling a catch in his throat. It was something he had wanted, and now it was so. At the same instant, he thought about Richard Chong.

"Uh," Josh began, glancing at his father and Tank. "Dad told me that—I mean..." He floundered and stopped.

Mr. Ladd cleared his throat and said, "We heard on the television news that..." He hesitated.

Duke spoke quickly. "We know. The police found the stretch limo sticking out of the water near a cane field on the north shore." He took a deep breath and continued, "I would have liked for things to be different, but they weren't. I hoped he would change, but, well, he chose not to.

"Now he's gone, and I'm sorry, but I'm also free. I, too, have made a choice. I won't be the wild surfer anymore. I want to stick around so Kekoa and I can make up for the lost years when he had no grandson and I had no caring grandfather."

"And I want to do the same, of course," Kekoa said softly. "Duke and I were talking just before you came up. Such things as tidal waves make one philosophical, I suppose. I remembered hearing there is something in your sacred writings about reaping what you sow, is there not?"

Josh nodded, remembering the verse in Galatians 6. He also remembered his thoughts at the ancient lava flow behind the church. Again, God had brought order out of chaos, showing He was sovereign.

"The law of getting what you plant works both ways," Josh observed.

"How so?" Duke asked.

"Well, I wanted to solve the mystery of Hidden Cove and to get you two together. I did everything I could to make that happen. It looked pretty hopeless for a while, but now. . ."

Josh hesitated, then added, "I would never have figured it would take a tidal wave to make it come true, but it happened. So the law of getting what you plant is a good one to remember."

After everyone nodded in agreement, Tank asked, "What will you two do now?"

Duke and Kekoa looked at each other before answering. "Well, school starts in a couple of weeks," Duke said, "and we've got a lot of things to do before then. There are many legal problems, as I'm sure you'd guess, about making Kekoa my guardian and so forth."

"In the meantime, my most welcome friends," Kekoa said, "we would be honored if you joined us for dinner." He pointed inland. "My home is small and humble, but it's safe, well above the tidal wave's reach."

"Thanks," Josh said, smiling happily, "but how about you both come up to our place instead?" He glanced at his father. "Wouldn't that be okay, Dad?"

Mr. Ladd nodded and said, "I'm sure your mother would be honored to have such guests, as I would be."

"That way," Josh added, "both of you can have an instant extended calabash family. I mean, counting mine, Tank's and all the others in our neighborhood."

"We accept!" Kekoa exclaimed, glancing at Duke, who

nodded. "We will have much to talk about!"

Josh's father grinned. "Let's get started," he said. "And while we're walking back up to my car, I hope you two will persuade my son and his friend Tank here to put adventures and mysteries aside and concentrate on school for a while."

"Well, Dad," Josh said with a broad smile, "I'll think about that. But we won't guarantee anything, will we, Tank?"

"No, but I'm sure it's going to be an interesting school year," Tank replied.

"For all of us!" Duke exclaimed.

"For all of us!" Kekoa echoed emphatically.

The men and boys turned inland toward the kiawe,* laughing and talking. They didn't look back. Hidden Cove held no secret now. It would no longer be kapu.*

The five friends climbed upward toward Diamond Head and a future bright with promise for everyone.

GLOSSARY

Chapter One

Aloha shirt: (*ah-low-hah*) A loose-fitting man's Hawaiian shirt worn outside the pants. The garment is usually very colorful.

Freeze frame: A single frame, or photograph, taken from a video tape.

Haole: (*how-lee*) A Hawaiian word originally meaning "stranger" but now used to mean Caucasian, or white person.

Oahu: (*ah-wah-hoo*) Hawaii's most populous island and the site of its capital city, Honolulu.

Pidgin English: (*pidj-uhn*) A simplified version of English. It was originally used in the Orient for communication between people who spoke different languages.

Sea urchin: An animal with a thin shell that's covered with sharp, movable spines.

Skeg: A fin on the rear bottom of a surfboard that's used for steering and stability. Modern surfboards often have two or three fins.

Still camera: A camera that takes conventional, nonmoving pictures, as opposed to a video or movie camera.

Zinc oxide: An ointment used to treat sunburn.

Chapter Two

Board and batten house: A house with a particular style of siding. Wide boards or sheets of lumber are set vertically, and the joints are covered by small strips of wood (battens).

Diamond Head: The 760-foot extinct volcano at the east end of Honolulu. It's the most famous landmark in Hawaii.

Haole: (*how-lee*) A Hawaiian word originally meaning "stranger" but now used to mean Caucasian, or white person.

Hapahaole: (*ha-pa-how-lee*) A person who's part Caucasian, part nonwhite.

Ironwood tree: A leafless tree with long, drooping, green needles. Sometimes called an Australian pine, in Hawaii this tree is used as a windbreak. Ironwood is sometimes cut and shaped like high hedges.

Kapu: (*kah-poo*) A Hawaiian warning that means "taboo, forbidden, keep out."

Kauai: (*cow-eye*) A Hawaiian island northwest of Oahu. Kauai is thought by many to be the most photogenic of the islands.

Kiawe: (*kee-ah-vay*) A thorny tree that can grow as tall as a house.

Malihini: (*mah-lee-hee-nee*) Hawaiian for "newcomer."

Waikiki: (*wai-kee-kee*) Honolulu's famous beach and resort area.

Zoris: (*zor-eez*) Flat, thonged sandals usually made of straw, leather or rubber.

Chapter Three

Akamai: (*ah-kah-my*) Hawaiian for "smart, intelligent."

Akamu: (*ah-kah-moo*) Hawaiian for "Adam."

Aloha: (*ah-low-hah*) A practical Hawaiian word with varied meanings, including "hello," "good-bye" and "love."

Aloha shirt: (*ah-low-hah*) A loose-fitting man's Hawaiian shirt worn outside the pants. The garment is usually very colorful.

Be-still tree: A short, poisonous tree with dense, green foliage and bright yellow flowers that fold up at night.

Haole: (*how-lee*) A Hawaiian word originally meaning "stranger" but now used to mean Caucasian, or white person.

Hilo: (*hee-low*) Capital city and port on the Big Island of Hawaii. Located on the northeast coast.

Hokkaido: (*hoe-kide-oh*) Northernmost of the main

Japanese islands.

Kabuki doll: (*kuh-boo-kee*) A doll made up to look like one of the highly stylized dancers of traditional Japanese drama.

Kahuna: (*kah-hoo-nah*) A Hawaiian priest representing the ancient or traditional beliefs.

Kalakaua Avenue: (*kah-lah-cow-ah*) The main street running through Waikiki.

Kanaka: (*kah-nah-kah*) A native Hawaiian man.

Kapu: (*kah-poo*) A Hawaiian warning that means "taboo, forbidden, keep out."

Kiawe: (*kee-ah-vay*) A thorny tree that can grow as tall as a house.

Kurils: (*kyur-eels*) A chain of small islands off the eastern coast of the U.S.S.R. and north of Japan. Under Soviet control since 1945.

Lanai: (*la-nye*) A patio, porch or balcony. Also the name of a small Hawaiian island west of Maui.

Malihini: (*mah-lee-hee-nee*) Hawaiian for "newcomer."

Muumuu: (*moo-oo-moo-oo*) A loose, colorful dress or gown frequently worn by women in Hawaii. This word is sometimes mispronounced "moo-moo."

Mynah: (*my-nah*) An Asian starling that's dark brown and black and has a white tail tip and wing markings, with a bright yellow bill and feet.

Oahu: (*ah-wah-hoo*) Hawaii's most populous island

145

and the site of its capital city, Honolulu.

Oleander: (*oh-lee-an-der*) A poisonous evergreen shrub with fragrant flowers in white, pink or red.

Plumeria: (*ploo-mar-ee-ah*) A shrub or small tree that produces large, fragrant blossoms often used to make leis (flower wreaths or necklaces).

Pupule: (*poo-poo-lay*) Hawaiian for "crazy."

Richter Scale: (*rik-ter*) A scale scientists use to express the size of an earthquake. A 2.0 is the smallest quake that can be felt; a 4.5 is a quake that causes slight damage; an 8.5 is a devastating quake.

Samurai: (*sam-ah-rye*) Part of the Japanese aristocracy.

Shoji screen: (*show-jee*) A wooden-framed paper screen, often decorated, used as a wall, partition or sliding door in Japanese homes.

Tsunami: (*tsoo-nahm-ee*) The Japanese word that in Hawaii means "tidal wave."

Waikiki: (*wai-kee-kee*) Honolulu's famous beach and resort area.

Chapter Four

Duke Kahanamoku: (*kah-ha-nah-mow-koo*) Hawaiian man who won the 100-meter freestyle swim in two Olympic games. He also popularized surfing.

Haole: (*how-lee*) A Hawaiian word originally meaning "stranger" but now used to mean Caucasian, or white person.

Kamaaina: (*kah-mah-eye-nah*) Hawaiian for "native" or "local person."

Kapu: (***kah**-poo*) A Hawaiian warning that means "taboo, forbidden, keep out."

Kauai: (*cow-eye*) A Hawaiian island northwest of Oahu. Kauai is thought by many to be the most photogenic of the islands.

Menehune: (*meh-nah-**hoo**-nay*) In this story, the word refers to children ages 3 to 13 who are eligible to enter a surfing competition held each October on Oahu. The word also refers to a race of tiny people in Hawaiian legends who are credited with building many temples, fishponds and roads. They worked only at night, and if their work was not completed in one night, it remained unfinished.

Oahu: (*ah-**wah**-hoo*) Hawaii's most populous island and the site of its capital city, Honolulu.

Pakalolo: (*pa-kah-low-low*) Hawaiian for "marijuana," an illegal drug.

Pupule: (*poo-**poo**-lay*) Hawaiian for "crazy."

Tsunami: (*tsoo-**nahm**-ee*) The Japanese word that in Hawaii means "tidal wave."

Waikiki: (***wai**-kee-kee*) Honolulu's famous beach and resort area.

Chapter Five
Banyan tree: (***ban**-yun*) A tree of the mulberry fam-

ily that extends shoots from its branches that drop to the ground and root, forming secondary trunks. A single banyan tree may cover several acres of ground.

Haole: (*how-lee*) A Hawaiian word originally meaning "stranger" but now used to mean Caucasian, or white person.

Kalakaua Avenue: (*kah-lah-cow-ah*) The main street running through Waikiki.

Pakalolo: (*pa-kah-low-low*) Hawaiian for "marijuana," an illegal drug.

Waikiki: (*wai-kee-kee*) Honolulu's famous beach and resort area.

Chapter Six

Lanai: (*la-nye*) A patio, porch or balcony. Also the name of a small Hawaiian island west of Maui.

Waikiki: (*wai-kee-kee*) Honolulu's famous beach and resort area.

Zoris: (*zor-eez*) Flat, thonged sandals usually made of straw, leather or rubber.

Chapter Seven

Alligator pear tree: A tropical tree also known as the avocado tree.

Beefsteak hedge: A hedge made up of beefsteak plants, which have red or purple foliage.

Bougainvillea: (*boo-gun-veel-ee-yah*) A tropical ornamental climbing vine with brilliant clusters of flowers. Colors include red, lavender and coral.

Hibiscus: (*high-bis-kus*) Hawaii's state flower. It has large, open blossoms available in many colors.

Kahuna: (*kah-hoo-nah*) A Hawaiian priest representing the ancient or traditional beliefs.

Mahalo: (*mah-ha-low*) Hawaiian for "thanks."

Makai: (*mah-kye*) Hawaiian word meaning "toward the sea."

Mango: A yellowish red tropical fruit and the evergreen tree that bears it.

Molokai: (*mow-low-kye*) The Hawaiian island directly east and a bit south of Oahu.

Monkeypod tree: An ornamental tropical tree that has clusters of flowers, sweet pods eaten by cattle and wood used in carving.

Moopuna: (*mow-oh-poo-nah*) Hawaiian for "grandchild."

Oahu: (*ah-wah-hoo*) Hawaii's most populous island and the site of its capital city, Honolulu.

Poi: (*poy*) A favorite Hawaiian dish made of paste from the taro plant. Many visitors say poi tastes like library paste.

Taro: (*tar-oh*) A plant grown throughout the tropics for its edible, starchy roots.

Tsunami: (*tsoo-nahm-ee*) The Japanese word that in Hawaii means "tidal wave."

Tutu: (*too-too*) Hawaiian for "grandmother."

Tutu makua: (*too-too-mah-***koo***-ah*) Hawaiian for "grandfather."

Chapter Eight

Banzai Pipeline: (*bahn-***zi***) A famous surfing area on the north shore of Oahu.

Kanaka: (*kah-***nah***-kah*) A native Hawaiian man.

Kiawe: (*kee-***ah***-vay*) A thorny tree that can grow as tall as a house.

Koolaus: (***koh***-oh-*lows*) The volcanic mountains that rise directly behind Honolulu.

Maui: (***mau***-ee*) Second largest of the main Hawaiian islands; 728 square miles in area.

Nahuna Point: (*nah-***hoo***-nah*) A point of land on the coast of Maui.

Waikiki: (***wai***-kee-***kee***) Honolulu's famous beach and resort area.

Waimea Bay: (*wai-***may***-ah*) A famous surfing area on the north shore of Oahu.

Chapter Nine

Akamu: (*ah-kah-***moo***) Hawaiian for "Adam."

Haole: (***how***-lee*) A Hawaiian word originally meaning "stranger" but now used to mean Caucasian, or white person.

Hilo: (***hee***-low*) Capital city and port on the Big Island of Hawaii. Located on the northeast coast.

Koko Head: (***ko***-ko*) An extinct volcano on the

southeast tip of Oahu.

Oahu: (*ah-wah-hoo*) Hawaii's most populous island and the site of its capital city, Honolulu.

Pakalolo: (*pa-kah-low-low*) Hawaiian for "marijuana," an illegal drug.

Tsunami: (*tsoo-nahm-ee*) The Japanese word that in Hawaii means "tidal wave."

Waikiki: (*wai-kee-kee*) Honolulu's famous beach and resort area.

Chapter Ten

Kiawe: (*kee-ah-vay*) A thorny tree that can grow as tall as a house.

Lanai: (*la-nye*) A patio, porch or balcony. Also the name of a small Hawaiian island west of Maui.

Pakalolo: (*pa-kah-low-low*) Hawaiian for "marijuana," an illegal drug.

Waikiki: (*wai-kee-kee*) Honolulu's famous beach and resort area.

Chapter Eleven

Kalakaua Avenue: (*kah-lah-cow-ah*) The main street running through Waikiki.

Mongoose: A small, agile mammal that feeds on birds' eggs and rodents.

Pakalolo: (*pa-kah-low-low*) Hawaiian for "marijuana," an illegal drug.

Tsunami: (*tsoo-nahm-ee*) The Japanese word that

in Hawaii means "tidal wave."
Waikiki: (*wai-kee-kee*) Honolulu's famous beach and resort area.

Chapter Twelve
Kiawe: (*kee-ah-vay*) A thorny tree that can grow as tall as a house.
Tsunami: (*tsoo-nahm-ee*) The Japanese word that in Hawaii means "tidal wave."

Chapter Thirteen
Aloha: (*ah-low-hah*) A practical Hawaiian word with varied meanings, including "hello," "goodbye" and "love."
Calabash: (*kal-ah-bash*) The gourd from which Hawaiians eat poi at a community dinner. A calabash grandfather would be an honorary grandfather.
Kahuna: (*kah-hoo-nah*) A Hawaiian priest representing the ancient or traditional beliefs.
Kapu: (*kah-poo*) A Hawaiian warning that means "taboo, forbidden, keep out."
Kiawe: (*kee-ah-vay*) A thorny tree that can grow as tall as a house.
Tsunami: (*tsoo-nahm-ee*) The Japanese word that in Hawaii means "tidal wave."
Tutu kane makua: (*too-too-kah-nee-mah-koo-ah*) Another Hawaiian term for "grandfather."